HER ROYAL BODYGUARD

A LESBIAN ROMANCE

MARGAUX FOX

1

"I'll make this very simple for you Alexandra," said her father, King George VII. A tall man, usually distant from his daughter, he sat across the large oak desk looking across it's rich leather top.

"You are a Princess. You are the heir to my throne. You must marry and bear children. No, it doesn't have to be Lord Hugo, but you must find someone suitable. I have had Henry draw up some suggestions and over the following weeks you will spend time with any that interest you. You will choose a husband. The future of the monarchy depends upon it."

Henry, her father's advisor, jumped in

with a thick folder which he handed to her. "Please take a good look Ma'am. We have done a lot of research on these men. I have included all the information I can. Please come to me if you have any questions or you don't like any of them, I will find more for you."

Henry was like an attentive dog in the way he followed her father around. He smoothed down his navy blue suit jacket with it's bold red lapels. Alexandra hated this new uniform the palace staff wore. She always thought the red lapels looked cheap.

Alexandra felt the burden of the throne yet again. The promise that, upon the death of her father, she would become Queen. It seemed sometimes like a joke. Like a fairytale. As though it was someone else's life than her own. But it wasn't. She had been carefully trained and prepared her whole life for her future. For her responsibilities that went beyond merely herself. She would become responsible for England, the United Kingdom and the countries of the Commonwealth.

As the only child of the King the pressure was all on her.

"You have a year." King George said. "A year from today, I will announce your marriage. You get to choose who. Obviously within the usual constraints. But please, Alexandra. You will without doubt become Queen. Our country is a mess. Nobody is happy with the Prime Minister or the political mess we are in. The people of our kingdom need you now. They need to see your strength, they need to see a Royal Wedding and a Royal Baby. They need to see your commitment to this monarchy's future. You are the darling of the media. You are the heir they want. Please, Alexandra Victoria, you are thirty four years old. This is your moment to shine. Give the people what they want."

Alexandra sat quietly, so much rushing through her quick mind.

"I was older when I married," he continued. "But it is different for men. I could still father children. There are things we must do in this life. There are burdens that we must bear, you and I, and my mother before us. Just us, the direct heirs. There are ways we must live and appearances we must keep up." He looked up to her.

"Sacrifices."

"Sacrifices, Alexandra. Our lives are not our own. We belong to the people. The throne will govern our choices. I know we have your eggs frozen and that buys us time and options, but there aren't endless years Alexandra. This is your duty. Do not let us down." His eyes were firm and stoic.

"I will look at my options Father." Alexandra gestured to the folder with her eyes. Duty bound her lips from saying the words she wanted to. The words she was thinking. She had called the meeting to say she wanted to end things with Lord Hugo. That she had never liked him especially. They had given her that permission, but followed it up with more pressure. More sacrifice required from her. An order to interview new potential husbands.

"Please do so, Alexandra."

"Thank you for your time Ma'am." Henry bowed his respect to his future Queen. He was about forty years old and the stress of his work had begun to tell around his eyes. He was beginning to look tired. Alexandra wondered if his respect for her was because he still wanted to work as the Monarch's right hand when her father died. Not that King George was dying. But he was seventy two now. He wouldn't live forever.

She would have a woman, she thought to herself. Obviously there was a tradition for Royal Advisors to be men. Not anymore. Queen Alexandra would have a right hand woman. It was 2020, times were changing.

Alexandra had begun to notice that as she grew into adulthood, she started to get her own way on a lot of things, as long as she didn't clash with her father. The monarchy may not have held the power that it used to years ago, but it still did hold power. Her's second only to her father's.

Alexandra nodded her respect and turned and left her father's study. Her chambermaid Jess waited outside for her and quickly fell in step next to her as she headed back to her own living quarters.

"Ma'am I have the copy of 'Hello' Magazine you requested, it is in your Drawing Room." Jess's tight navy waistcoat emphasising her slim waist and petite frame as she scuttled along next to Alexandra. New to Alexandra's household. Determined to be the most keen and the most helpful.

"Your clothes are pressed and laid out for your first appearance at the children's charity lunch. You need to be ready for 11.30am. Alicia is here to do hair and make-up. Natalie thought that neat blue McQueen dress would be ideal for today. Then you have the dinner with the Polish Ambassador tonight. Natalie has a dress by an up and coming Polish designer for you to wear and you will dine at the private room at the Ivy so that you can be photographed coming and going. They think it best for you to get some more exposure."

"Thank you Jess." Alexandra looked to her. Jess smiled and blushed, still not used to working for royalty. Every time overcome by the fact that someone as famous as Alexandra knew her name. Alexandra was one of the most photographed women in the world. One of the most loved celebrities. Always kind, always polite. Always supporting a range of charities.

Alexandra breezed back into her chambers and immediately slipped into the role she had been playing her whole life. Immediately into the Princess that people expected and wanted to see. She picked up 'Hello' magazine and slipped into the chair by the mirror where Alicia was waiting to do her hair.

"Good morning Alicia. Good morning Natalie."Alexandra smiled kindly to each woman in turn. Acknowledging their existence and the work that they did for her.

Alicia ran her fingers through Alexandra's ash blonde long bob. Alexandra regularly won magazine contests detailing the "Most Stylish Woman" or "Most Beautiful Woman" of the year. The media loved her and loved to take her photo. It wasn't hard to be beautiful and stylish when you had a team around you whose full time job it was to make sure you were the most beautiful and stylish at all times.

Alexandra often wished she could say publicly:

"It isn't true. None of this is real. I don't really look like this. Beauty isn't what really matters."

But it would be a lie. Beauty still did matter in this fucked up world that we lived in. It was still vitally important that Alexandra was always beautiful, always stylish.

Alicia worked away at Alexandra's hair. Alicia's father was African American and her mother was white and she grew up in a poor area of London. Alexandra chose to employ her because it was important to her that her staff reflected diversity. It was important that her staff weren't all white and middle class. Alicia wasn't chosen to be politically correct. Alicia was chosen because visibility matters. A mixed race working class girl in Alexandra's inner circle matters. It helps the people to believe. Alicia was great at her job. But lots of girls were. There could be hundreds of suitable candidates for hair and make up for the future Queen of England. But Alicia it was.

Alexandra thumbed through the pages of the magazine. 'Hello' was always the magazine of choice for Royal features. They had run a feature on Alexandra's work in a cancer hospice. Photos of Alexandra with the cancer patients. Alexandra sitting at their bedside, talking gently to them. Alexandra playing games with them, laughing with them. Alexandra making them feel human again. It did the image of the Royal Family a lot of good to cultivate their *'Perfect Princess'*. Alexandra, Princess of the people. Alexandra, always lovely, she could connect with anyone.

Alexandra turned the page. The photographers had captured her holding the hand of a dying woman.

Olivia

Alexandra remembered her name. She always would. Olivia's gaunt eyebrow and eyelash-less face under the headscarf. Olivia was the same age as Alexandra and had a new husband and a baby. She had spoken of the things she wished she could have done, the life she wished she could have lived. How she wished so much she could live to see her baby grow up. But it was taken away from her. She was only thirty four years old. Alexandra had written a card to her the following day and asked her staff to keep her appraised of Olivia's condition. It was only a week later when she was informed that Olivia had died.

There it was, life and death; that quick and easy stroke that could happen to any of us at any time.

Yet, here was Olivia, forever immortalised in a photograph with Princess Alexandra. Olivia dying in bed and Alexandra sitting next to her holding her hand. Alexandra's own face kind and gentle. A tear on Alexandra's cheek. Was that real? Did they photoshop it? It was an iconic photograph that Alexandra knew would raise her status. A photograph that would be all over social media by now. The ever loving Alexandra with her kind open heart. The image of herself that had been cultivated carefully by the palace's press and media department since she was a child.

Princess Alexandra the good.

Princess Alexandra would be a brighter future.

Queen Alexandra one day.

Polls said she would be far more popular as a monarch than her father had ever been.

The public loved Alexandra and demanded more and more from her.

Alexandra looked at her blue eyes in the mirror, her ash blonde hair full around her face with Alicia's work. Her make up immaculate. Small tasteful diamonds glinting at her ears and neck.

She was the Princess the people demanded. Every year she gave more of herself and it was never enough. Could she feign a marriage to a suitable man just to make the people happy?

She had one year to do it. To find a man to marry. To give the people the Royal Wedding that they wanted.

Alexandra sighed as she got up and went to her dressing room to put on her perfect outfit.

Her life was not her own.

2

Sergeant Erin Kennedy was part of branch SO14 Royalty Protection in the Metropolitan Police. She was just getting her breath back after a tough gym session following a nightshift. She had been working on Residential Security at one of the Royal Country Residences. A big country castle with none of the Royal family currently in it. Sure, a great use of highly trained royalty protection officers she always thought. She was frustrated by how boring Residential Security actually was. A glorified security guard.

Sweat dripped off her face and between her breasts under her police T shirt. As usual, she had trained hard. Her dark hair damp to her head and her face red with exertion.

"Kennedy. Get over here." Inspector Colin Travis shouted from the padded matting. He was the lead on unarmed combat. He was a tall, muscular guy with a bald head and intense blue eyes. He moved straight to a recap of things they had done before. He went to attack Erin from different angles with different weapons or methods of attack and every time her body reacted quickly and immediately diffused the threat.

"Very good Kennedy. Very Good," he said. "Now we are going to run through a defence from a handbag snatch.

Erin watched him as he asked her to pretend to grab the handbag from the training dummy. He went through the moves she needed to make to defend it. She always enjoyed unarmed combat. She had had times when Colin had thrown her to the floor and looked at her with those intense blue eyes that she had felt almost heterosexual. There was an intensity to his grip and his moves. She learnt to replicate them exactly. He was a very good teacher.

She finished up her training and then headed to shower and change and ordered a taxi to the train station to head home.

She made it home to her West London apartment later that day. It was grey and raining outside. The nature of her work was antisocial. She had 3 days off now. A Monday, Tuesday and Wednesday. Her few friends worked normal office hours so were nowhere to be seen.

Erin flicked the kettle on and settled on the sofa, contemplating her life choices. The Royalty Protection Unit had sounded prestigious and exciting. But it wasn't proving to be. It was taking up most of her life and her days off she often spent bored and lonely.

Her phone beeped and a voicemail flashed up. She swiped to listen to it.

Erin sweetheart, it's Mum. Your father and I were wondering when you are going to visit us. It has been such a long time since we have seen you.

Erin groaned and deleted it. She didn't have a great relationship with her parents. They had never loved the fact that their errant daughter was gay. Unmarried. No children. They ploughed all their energy into their golden son- Erin's brother Jack who had done exactly what was expected of him. Good job, nice but bland wife, two children. They had never appreciated Erin's job.

"Erin, darling. It is no job for a woman, the police in London. Why must you insist on doing such a manly job?" Erin's mother was patronising and painfully middle class. Nothing Erin did or said would ever make her parents happy.

Her phone beeped again. A text.

Babe, just wondering if you are home tonight? I could come over. x

Erin's on/off on/off girlfriend Sophie. Girlfriend really wasn't the right word. On/off because she couldn't decide what she wanted. Sophie was twenty nine years old and still had no idea what she wanted. A man or a woman? A relationship or not a relationship? Sophie changed her jobs as regularly as she changed her boyfriends and girlfriends. Sophie was charming and lovely and pretty but entirely unreliable as a partner. But then, Erin wasn't so sure she really wanted a long term partner anymore so maybe it was fine.

Erin did know that Sophie's text still had the ability to interest her straight away. It had been a while since she had had sex and Sophie could always be relied upon for a hot night, if nothing else.

She caught her fingers involuntarily typing in response.

Sure, come round for 7. Wear red underwear.

Company. Sex. A way through a miserable Monday evening. Better than another evening alone.

Erin took the opportunity to catch up on some sleep and set an alarm so she would be up when Sophie came over.

A dumb decision perhaps. She hoped Sophie wasn't going to bring drama with her.

ERIN'S ALARM woke her and she stretched in bed, yawning. Her muscular body naked and pale from the winter. She got up and pulled on some underwear and a black vest with no bra. Her dark hair was a long tangle so she dragged a brush through it and spritzed herself with her favourite scent. It was an androgynous perfume, mostly masculine, a little feminine. It was enough, she thought as she looked in the mirror, her eyes dark and dangerous. There was no need for more clothes. She wouldn't be wearing them long enough.

Sophie was late. Unsurprisingly. But at 7.40 the doorbell rang. Erin answered it. There was Sophie. Dazzling. Heels and a long coat. A cloud of scent and long blonde curls. Erin's lonely flat suddenly was alive again.

"Hey," Sophie said as she breezed in. "You look great."

Then she removed her coat and there she was just in red lace underwear and heels. Her body all the curves and perfection of a swimwear model. Her heels gave her the appearance of a porn star.

Erin knew she would leave the heels on while they fucked. Sophie knew Erin liked the look. And Sophie lived for attention. Sophie shone for people wanting her.

Erin always wanted her.

Erin was all over her straight away, Sophie pushed back onto the sofa, her wet underwear pushed to the side as Erin was on top of her and thrusting her fingers into her. Sophie bit into Erin's shoulder as she took it. Hard, passionate, relieving the frustrations of them both. They were ready, they were both so ready. Erin felt Sophie's orgasm all over her hand and underneath her body. Sophie had this gift of never really tiring of sex, this insatiable need. She would come and then seconds later, she would want fucking again. More, harder. And the cycle would repeat. The sex between Erin and Sophie was very much one way. It always had been. But Erin didn't mind that. It meant she never had to be vulnerable. Moving Sophie's beautiful body as she wanted her, taking her in different positions, every which way. Moving location, all over the apartment. Sophie still loving it, Sophie vocal and appreciative. God knows what the neighbours thought. The walls were paper thin.

Erin didn't care. She always felt like she was in a porn film when she had sex with Sophie. It was just what she needed. Sophie eventually lay satiated on the bed in a wet patch, her hair a mess and her underwear round her knees. Erin put her fingers in her own underwear and finished herself in seconds. Just looking at a well fucked Sophie was more than enough to bring her to orgasm.

Erin got straight up and into the shower. The power of the water rushing down onto her face as she closed her eyes and raised her head to the water.

Erin dried herself off and headed to the fridge in a towel. She went back to the bedroom with two beers. Sophie sat up in bed and took the offered bottle of beer.

Taking a big gulp of it, she said to Erin, "Thanks so much. I needed that. I feel so much better for it."

And Erin did too. The sex, the beer. So many frustrations eased out.

"So, how's life?" Erin asked.

"Oh, you know. Messy. Complicated. I've kind of been seeing this guy. But the sex is rubbish. I met a married couple on-line too and I am thinking of seeing them both together. Oh and I have started out as a self employed make up artist for weddings and things and I quit my other job. I mean I know I'm not OFFICIALLY a make up artist. But, I can do make up. So I figured, why get hung up on technicalities? So yeah, I'm trying to get some bookings. Struggling for money a bit, but you know how it is."

That was Sophie all over. Erin sighed and realised that actually, sex with Sophie was more than enough.

Sophie left later on and Erin was enjoying another beer to herself. She had put fresh sheets on her bed and was just putting the sexed up sheets in the washing machine when her phone rang.

"Sergeant Kennedy?" a male voice said sternly.

"Yes," she replied.

"Chief Inspector Randle here. There's been an accident. Princess Alexandra's Personal Protection Officer has been injured. The Princess needs a female replacement. I need you to meet her and interview at Buckingham Palace tomorrow morning at 10am."

It wasn't a question. It was an order. He knew damn well that no officer on a shitty residential security job would think twice when offered the chance to work on the heir to the British throne.

"I'll be there," said Erin.

3

It was another grey drizzly morning as Erin in her smartest dark blue trouser suit waited at Buckingham Palace for Princess Alexandra to appear. The opulence and grandeur of the decor didn't faze her. Since working on the palaces and castles belonging to the Royal Family, Erin was no longer surprised by the decadence both interior and exterior. It had become a strange sort of normality, working in these palaces for these people. People just like us, but different. Born to nobility, to royalty. People whose destiny from birth was one of a regal nature.

Erin had read and heard a lot about

Princess Alexandra although she always preferred to meet someone and judge them for herself. Princess Alexandra's reputation of loveliness preceded her.

Erin picked up a copy of Hello Magazine from the table and scanned through it. Princess Alexandra holding the hand of a dying woman, a tear glistening in her eye. Could anyone really be as compassionate, as perfect as this woman was made out to be? What were her secrets? There must be some, hiding behind the perfection. Erin might get the chance to know the real Alexandra.

Erin stood as a member of the Princess's staff approached. A petite girl in a waistcoat who barely looked old enough to be working for anyone, her hair immaculately twisted into a bun, her make up understated.

"Princess Alexandra will see you now," said the girl and she turned and motioned for Erin to follow her. Erin fell into step behind the girl whose short legs moved quickly as though she had somewhere important to be. Which she did really, at the beck and call of the future Queen.

Erin followed the slim girl into the Princess's drawing room. A big room with lovely wide windows overlooking the garden, a large ornate sofa and elegant chairs around a coffee table were the feature.

Alexandra stood up as Erin entered. She was every bit as beautiful as her photographs and there was a moment, just a moment where Erin just gazed at the loveliness of her face before she remembered herself and where she was.

Erin curtsied to her. A curtsy was a bizarre and sexist tradition and show of respect which didn't work quite so well in the trousers Erin was wearing. They felt a touch on the tight side after Christmas indulgences and there was no give as Erin moved one foot backwards and dropped down into the curtsy nodding her head.

"Your Royal Highness." Erin greeted Alexandra.

"Welcome, Sergeant Kennedy," said Alexandra her voice dripping with privilege and importance. She approached and shook Erin's hand. Her hand as elegant as the rest of her, fingers long and slim, nails neat and with a natural french manicure.

Erin held her strong gaze without looking away.

"You can call me Erin," Erin replied boldly. Alexandra raised an eyebrow. "If you want, I mean," she added hastily.

Erin wasn't expecting the effect that Alexandra would have on her. But she took a deep breath and pulled herself together.

"Please sit," said Alexandra.

Erin sat opposite Alexandra and Alexandra summoned the petite girl that had brought her through to organise tea for them both.

"Thank you for coming on such short notice Erin. Now, I don't want to waste your time or my own, so I will get to the finer points of what I need in my personal body-guard." Alexandra's voice was kind, but firm and Erin appreciated her directness.

"Of course," replied Erin.

"Firstly, I need someone dedicated. I need someone who can live my life with me, be my shadow. You will be given time off, scheduled carefully of course and you will be compensated well. But, as I am sure you are aware, along with my increasing status, there comes increased risk with everything I do. I want to trust one person implicitly with my life. I don't want to chop and change my personal protection regularly."

Erin knew exactly what she was asking. They say a truly great bodyguard should be the 'Grey Man' or in this case 'Grey Woman'. They should become the shadow of the star, always there, never noticed. The Princess wanted her own shadow, she wanted to look behind her and know whose eyes she would see and they would reassure her. This was often the case with a female client, they liked to know who was looking after them, they wanted to know and trust their protection. A male client, more commonly, could have one of twenty protection officers working one to one with them and they wouldn't care, but Alexandra wanted a face she would know to be with her at all times.

"I've had a couple of incidents lately, as I am sure you have been briefed upon, with over zealous members of the public and then separately, there has been an assassination threatened by terrorists. Obviously our security services are looking closely at this assassination threat and there is nothing currently to verify it, but we have to be aware that it is there." Alexandra's beautiful face in the light was solemn and serious. Erin obviously had been briefed on the threats on the Princess and the level of risk but was surprised that the security service had told Alexandra herself.

"You look surprised," Alexandra said and she smiled. "You think they wouldn't tell me the serious stuff?"

"Er... no. Well.. yes. I am surprised. Usually we don't tell the client," stammered Erin.

There was a knock at the door and the tea arrived on a trolley pushed by a waist-coated waiter. There was silence as he served the tea to them both and then left.

"I need to know, Erin. It is imperative that I know everything. It is imperative that I trust you implicitly and that if I ask you something, anything, I get an honest answer. I know there is a risk attached purely to my name, to who I am and the life I was born into. I want to be the best I can be and do good things with my name and status. Make a difference to the lives of people, in both our own country and those less privileged. If the price I pay for the good that I do ends up being my life, I am okay with that. But I want to work with someone who will give me all the information, someone who will protect me, but also advise me and help me make choices. Can you be that person?"

"I can always be honest with you, yes," replied Erin.

"Good," said Alexandra. "My other requirement is that you don't have family, a partner, children? I don't want to take you away from your family. I need to be able to be selfish at times. I need someone who can become part of my life. Do you have children Erin?"

"No."

"A partner?" asked Alexandra.

Erin thought for a moment about Sophie. Hot Sophie. Sexy Sophie and all the wild sex they had had.

Then she thought about her loneliness and her sad apartment.

"Um....no."

"So you could dedicate your life to me?" asked the Princess. "I cannot ask you for forever, but for a few years at least. Be with me, be by my side, be the one I look to and trust with my life."

"Yes." Erin said, wishing she had some more words. But she didn't. Alexandra kept fixing her with those intense blue eyes and Erin was lost for words.

"Erin, another thing, can you ride horses? Your resume said you could, but I really need to be sure. I often ride when I can and I like to ride other places than just the palace grounds. I like to ride fast and I like to jump whatever I can. I am very limited on this if I don't have personal security that can keep up with me. My last bodyguard had an accident falling from the horse."

Erin smiled. For once, something she was confident at.

"Sure, I grew up riding and I actually used to work with horses before I was in the police. I worked for an Event rider. Riding horses, galloping and jumping, for me is as easy as walking on my own feet."

Alexandra smiled widely. The smile that newspapers around the world loved to capture.

"Oh wonderful. I can't wait to get back out there. I have some lovely horses. I'm sure you will find one that you like."

Alexandra's expression changed suddenly and she became serious again. "Erin, I would love to take you on to work for me. There is one more thing. I know you will be made to sign further Non Disclosure Agreements before starting with me, but there are times I will ask you for complete confidentiality on my movements. Not just regarding public disclosure but also regarding disclosure to other members of the Royal Family, my father-the king. Sometimes I will even ask you for confidentiality from the rest of the security team, from your boss, confidentiality from everyone. Can you make me that promise?" Alexandra looked earnest and almost vulnerable as she asked.

What secrets was she hiding, Erin wondered. Promising to keep secrets from the rest of the security team and her boss went against all of her training. Promising to keep too many secrets was a really bad idea. Alexandra obviously went to places she didn't want anyone to know about. But, in reality, how much risk was attached to this?

Before she could stop herself, Erin had replied. "Sure. I promise. Whatever confidentiality you need, you have it. You have my word."

Their eyes connected and Alexandra smiled and stood up.

"Thank you very much Erin."

"JESS," she called out towards the door.

The door opened and an over keen Jess practically ran into the room.

"Yes Ma'am," said Jess quickly.

"Organise for Sergeant Kennedy's belongings to be moved into my adjoining suite as a matter of priority."

"Sergeant Kennedy, you will start with me tomorrow morning. My security team will brief you and give you my schedule. Jess, please show Sergeant Kennedy out."

Just like that, Erin was given the biggest promotion there was in her line of work. Erin smiled to herself as she followed little Jess out. Protection of one of the most famous women in the world. This was exactly what she had trained for.

4

Erin was at the palace for 7am the next morning. Her clothes and belongings, not that there were a lot of them, were being moved for her. She met the rest of the Princess's security team at the Security offices.

"Sergeant Kennedy, great to see you." boomed the voice of a big bald headed man in a dark suit, every inch the stereotypical bodyguard image. "I'm Chief Inspector Mark Evans. I realise this is your first real Close Protection job, but we were really struggling to find a female officer that Rose would accept and that could damn well ride horses as well as she wants them to.

We have better officers than you and we have tried to train them to ride to the desired standard but it seems it is a skill required over years, not something that we can get someone up to speed with in a couple of months. "

"Rose?" Erin asked, confused.

"Rose is Princess Alexandra's Code Name. We always refer to her as Rose internally and on phone/radio et cetera for safety."

"Please tell me you weren't lying or exaggerating when you said you can ride to a high level?" he said.

"Not at all," replied Erin. "I've done it all my life. The riding will be no problem at all."

"Thank fuck for that. I can't have any more officers with broken legs. No fucking use to me with broken legs." Erin remained reserved. She couldn't tell if Chief Inspector Evans was serious.

"You can laugh you know. I am funny," he said.

"Sure," replied Erin cringing for him.

"Anyway. You weren't my choice, but you are hers, and one way or another, she outranks me. I could list fifty male officers who would be a far better choice, however she wants a female who can ride so we are stuck with you. All we can hope is that your ineptitude doesn't get the future queen of our country fucking killed. Capisce?"

Erin despised his use of the Italian word for effect, she hated his patronising attitude towards her, she hated his big shiny sweaty face. But she figured he would desire a response.

"Sure, I've got it."

"Here is the current folder on Rose, her likes, dislikes, her public schedule for the next month, past issues, current issues, her drivers, her cars, her team, everything about them. I suggest you take it away and get reading. We will run a briefing for the team every morning at 7am on the day ahead. Following that I will arrange for a 1:1 for you every morning with an experienced Close Protection officer so we are constantly upskilling you. We need you to be the best, which we obviously cannot achieve but let's hope for her sake we can get you up to a vaguely passable standard."

"This morning you will have Firearms

training with me. Rose won't be moving until this afternoon so I'll take you out to the range and see if you can shoot."

"Sure," replied Erin.

I'll show you I can damn well shoot, she thought to herself. I am SO much better than you think I am.

Hours later and Erin had managed to shoot *'pretty well for a beginner'* according to Evans, so she was beginning to prove herself slowly but surely.

Alexandra's schedule said she was leaving for horse riding at 2pm so Erin got ready for 1.30pm. She wore her riding clothes and pulled on the shoulder holster for her 9mm Glock 17 pistol. She fed her earpiece radio wire through the sleeve of the jacket they had given her to the wrist and then put it on covering the gun. People in the UK are always shocked by guns. Erin had been trained to keep her weapon concealed. Her riding hat and a change of clothes were in a bag she asked Jess to have taken down to the cars. She looked in the mirror and took a deep breath. She was ready. First day as bodyguard to the future Queen. She smiled. She figured the riding might be a test, so she was ready for whatever Alexandra had to throw at her.

Alexandra swept out of her apartment at 2pm exactly.

"Good afternoon Erin," she said.

"Good afternoon Ma'am," Erin replied and she fell into step behind Alexandra. She lifted her wrist and the microphone for her radio to her lips and spoke quietly:

"This is Kennedy. Rose is on the move. Over."

She heard the response immediately from James the driver:

"Roger. We are ready to go. Over"

They headed down the wide staircase, through the grand hallway, out of the main palace doors. The three black Range Rovers waited patiently. James was holding open the back door of the second vehicle. Alexandra got in the back of the Range

Rover and Erin got in the front passenger seat. James got into the driver's seat.

"Good afternoon Ma'am." said James jovially. "Everything as the schedule for this afternoon?"

"Please, James," Alexandra responded.

James started the car and Erin spoke into the radio:

"This is Kennedy. Rose is moving as per the schedule. Over."

Then they set off. So far, so good, thought Erin. Everything going smoothly. There was a lot more to Close Protection than most people realised. It wasn't about running round with a gun, taking out the bad guys as if you were in a movie. So much of it was the complex dance of radio transmissions, working with your team, informing your back up of your moves, making sure you didn't impede on the Princess's life any more than was absolutely necessary. Planning ahead to avoid danger, being extremely vigilant at all times. Very rarely were you expected to fight or shoot. But, if you did need to, you had better hope your skills were up to scratch or everything would end badly. Very, very badly.

They arrived at a large hilly woodland owned by the Royal Family. There was a horse box there and two stable girls standing outside of it holding beautiful horses. A small, compact grey horse and a big rangy looking chestnut. The horses wore saddles and bridles ready and the stable girls huddled in coats and scarves against the cold wind. Erin had studied maps of the woodland, memorised all the tracks. Studied Google Earth to try and get a handle on the many tracks, but she knew that she wouldn't know it quite well enough yet. Not until she had been round in person. There were two GPS wristbands she had been issued with. A silver one engraved with '*Rose*', she handed to Alexandra as they got out of the car.

"Thank you Sergeant Kennedy," said Alexandra.

The other one, Erin snapped onto her own wrist.

The back up team would follow their GPS location and make sure the cars were moved to the nearest pick up point. It was

Erin's job to know the fastest way to the cars at any point. Erin's job to watch for danger and to keep in radio contact with the back up.

"Good afternoon Paige. Good afternoon Michelle." Alexandra remembered the names of the stable girls too. It was astounding, Erin thought. She remembered everyone's names, or perhaps she had Jess brief her on which staff she would see each day, so it looked like she remembered their names. Either way, it made everyone feel special. It made everyone feel that bit of warm Princess Alexandra magic.

"This is Amber." Alexandra gestured to the chestnut horse as she spoke to Erin. "You will ride her."

Erin nodded and mounted the lovely Amber whilst Alexandra mounted the dazzlingly white horse. Erin wondered how many hours and what special shampoos it had taken the stable girls to make the white horse so clean.

And then they were off. Riding away from everyone. Erin felt nervous. Not of the riding, that bit was easy and comfortable for her, just nervous that she did everything right. She knew as the new girl and as a woman she would be constantly having to prove herself. She rode slightly to the side and behind Alexandra, giving her her space, still not knowing exactly how Alexandra liked everything. It was one thing reading and learning Alexandra's preferences but another to actually work so closely with one of the most famous women in the world.

Erin's horse was beautifully trained, it was obvious as soon as they set off. The mare was light in the hand and responsive to the leg. It was a pleasure to ride such a lovely horse.

Alexandra turned around in the saddle and looked back to Erin.

"Erin, please ride beside me."

"Of course Ma'am."

Erin moved her horse alongside Alexandra's.

"Erin, where did you learn to ride?" Alexandra asked, her eyes focussed on Erin as she asked.

Erin felt this strange nervousness again as Alexandra spoke to her.

"So I always rode. As a child, I guess.

My mum had horses. She borrowed this fat black pony for me to ride. He was called Tommy and he always had a look on his little face like he couldn't decide if he was going to throw me off or not that day."

Alexandra laughed, her smile wide and open. Her teeth perfect, neat and white.

"He was pretty naughty. I fell off a lot. She got me lessons and I got better. I guess I had to. You soon learn to hold on with a pony like that. I was obsessed with the horses. When I was a bit bigger and fell off less often, I would ride my mum's horses. We went to jumping competitions, sometimes we did pretty well. I always wanted to work with horses actually. I wanted to ride in the Olympics."

"Yet, here you are, babysitting members of the Royal Family? How did that happen? This won't help you get to the Olympics," Alexandra responded, she seemed genuinely curious.

"Oh, I did work with horses before I joined the police. I worked for an International Event Rider. She was in the British team. I learnt a lot. I loved it, mostly. The winters can be long and cold. But in the summer, it was the best job in the world. Riding beautiful horses in the sunshine."

"And the Olympics?" Alexandra asked.

"Oh, so I wasn't ever really good enough and I never had the right horse. I mean, I competed to a decent level. I maybe could have gone further. My best horse got seriously injured. It was a struggle to get by financially. I could train young horses, but then it made more sense financially to sell them, rather than risk them getting injured pursuing my selfish dreams. I could have done more. I could have dedicated years and years more of my life in the hope it came off. Working with horses is a long hard slog on an uneven field. They say it is a rich person's sport. And I was never a rich person. And I didn't have a rich family or husband to support me. I just loved the horses." Erin felt herself opening up. "I don't know, I have some regrets. Sometimes, I think I should have tried harder. Should have been more resilient, tougher. When things went wrong, I gave up and applied for the police."

It seemed somehow easy to talk suddenly. Erin found herself speaking words she had never spoken in the easy January air. A crisp winter's day they would call it. The sunshine lazy, but bright over the hillside. The grass dewy beneath the regular step of the hooves of the two horses and the only sounds, the birds in the trees and the rhythmic breath of the big beautiful animals.

It felt like they were the only two people in the world, the Princess and her bodyguard.

"Your best horse?"Alexandra asked. "What happened to her?"

"She died,"Erin said. Factual and distant to minimise the pain she had been through. "We had a really bad fall over a jump in a big competition and she broke her leg and had to be put to sleep. Well, they like to say put to sleep. They shoot them though, horses. They had to shoot her- she could never have recovered."

"Oh Erin, I am so sorry. I can't imagine how hard that was for you. What was her name? What was she like?" Alexandra asked.

Erin smiled, tiny tears threatening the

corner of her eyes. Nobody ever really asked that. When they found out the horse was dead, they changed the subject fast.

"Her name was Alaska. She was a big independent mare. She was fast and bold and an incredible jumper. Her bravery was probably what went wrong in the end, she was too brave and thought she knew it all. She misjudged the jump. Or I did. Or maybe we both did slightly. She liked apples better than carrots. She was the most intelligent horse I ever knew. I had her since she was young, we learned everything together."

"She was lucky to have you and lead the life she did, Erin. It sounds like a life of excitement and wonder. You should try to let go of blaming yourself." When Alexandra spoke, she spoke with a wisdom and balance beyond anything Erin had heard before.

Erin's radio crackled.

"Marshall to Kennedy. All OK? Over."

Erin woke up suddenly and put her wrist to her mouth.

"Affirmative Marshall. We are still heading South. Over."

Erin looked back to Alexandra, her position on the horse perfect, her hips moving with the horse and her hands light on the reins. The sunlight was on her face, lighting the perfect lines of her cheekbones. Her finely defined features golden in the light.

"Thank you Ma'am." Erin said. "Where did you learn to ride Ma'am."

"Oh, an almost similar story," Alexandra laughed. "My family always had horses. They got me a fat little pony when I was a child. He was less naughty than your Tommy by the sound of it." Alexandra laughed again. Her laughter was musical. She was angelic.

"The trouble with my family and my life is that I'm never allowed to fall. Not in any aspect of life. There's too many people saving me all of the time. I always loved the horses though. As a child I watched equestrian sports at the Olympics and I thought it was something I wanted to do when I grew up. That was before I really knew what 'Future Queen' meant. There are a lot of things you can't do as Future Queen. A lot of risks you cannot take. My cousin Zara rode in the Olympics you know?"

"Yes." Erin nodded.

"I was jealous of her. Jealous of her life and her world. The same, yet different. Zara was allowed to fall."

The two rode in silence for a minute, lovely horses stepping in time to each other.

"You want to canter up this hill?" Alexandra asked looking to Erin and smiling. "Race you," she said.

Before Erin could respond, Alexandra's heels were to her horses sides and the horse responded, powering up the hill. Erin urged her own horse forward worried for a second about the Princess's safety. Should she ride that fast? But as she chased her she saw Alexandra's perfect balance with the horse, she was a natural. There was nothing to worry about. She caught herself watching Alexandra's round ass bob up and down ahead of her in the tight breeches she was wearing. She shook her head and tried to come back to reality. This was work. This wasn't just a perv fest. She needed to stop being distracted by Alexandra. Somehow.

The wind was in their faces as the horses raced up the hill. It was exhilarating, fun. Erin could see why Alexandra needed the horses in her life. Riding was her freedom. The time when she could be really herself. At one with her horse. Once upon a time they were both pony-mad little girls. Just born into different worlds. Maybe Alexandra wasn't that different from her after all.

5

A couple of weeks passed and Erin began to get used to Alexandra's schedule. They settled into the dance of client and bodyguard. The bodyguard working to learn her client's every move, her every step, her every decision. Erin working to know exactly what the Princess wanted and needed before she knew it herself. Learning what scared the Princess, how present she wanted her protection in different situations. Still scanning constantly for danger. The only way to truly protect someone is to know them and their life better than you know your own.

Erin found herself easily slipping into the role of Alexandra's shadow. It was the most natural job she had ever found herself in. She was always alert and aware, but she blended easily into the background. Alexandra seemed happy with her. Alexandra began to be at ease and comfortable around her. Alexandra began to look to her for reassurance when they were out. Erin noticed a vulnerability in Alexandra that she would never have imagined was there.

There were walkabouts where they would visit cities and walk around meeting members of the public, Alexandra every inch the dazzling Princess they all wanted her to be.

There were charity events where Alexandra's face and presence would help the charity immeasurably. Erin watched from the sidelines as people took and took from Alexandra. Everyone wanted a piece of her, her time, her words, her touch. How much did she have to give? How long would she be able to keep giving?

When they finished for the day and re-

turned to one or other of Alexandra's residences, Erin would always walk with her
back to her suite of rooms- Erin's bedroom
and bathroom immediately next to the
Princess's. Alexandra would look tired then.
The loveliness of her face carried the great
burden of her role late in the evening in her
private rooms. She would kick off her heels
and sit quietly and sigh. Sometimes she
would request a drink or snack. Usually a
gin and tonic which would be brought to
her room quickly, a nervous waiter shy behind the trolley.

Alexandra always seemed to be alone in
the evening and late at night. Quiet, con-
templative and alone. Erin went to her own
room alone. She found herself more and
more distant from her own life and more
and more absorbed in the Princess's. She
ignored texts from Sophie. Sophie seemed
so insignificant suddenly. Sophie's beauty
that had always stunned her had paled in
her mind. She sat quietly and watched Netflix and read books.

She couldn't stop thinking about what
Alexandra might be doing behind the wall

that separated them. Alexandra sleeping, her face gentle in repose. Alexandra undressing, her skin golden in the warm light from her bedside lamp. Alexandra. Alexandra. Alexandra.

I can't stop thinking about you.

Six weeks after starting with Alexandra, Erin was settled into the routine. She attended the morning briefing at 7am each day with the security team. Half an hour every morning with Chief Inspector Evan's inflated ego and big shiny head was a necessary evil of the job. He might have a higher rank than her but she could see it constantly irked him that he wasn't in a more high profile position. He would never admit it but it was clear to Erin that he would have given anything to walk beside Alexandra or her father in public. He was the background man for the background men. He was stuck with organising and researching, sorting schedules, leading briefings, planning security advance parties for the venues Alexandra would visit.

The briefing was followed up with the promised daily 1:1 with an experienced officer. This particular day they ran through unarmed combat. Erin's muscle memory acting fast. Her reactions passing the tests they gave her. Her relief palpable. She was doing it. She was doing the job and doing it well. She was protecting the future Queen of the United Kingdom. So far, she had had zero fuck ups. So far, the officers doing the 1:1s with her were quietly impressed.

This was followed by her daily gym session in the palace gym. Fit for anything, that was what she was supposed to be. And she felt it. In the best shape she had been in. Her muscles lean and strong. Her body athletic, but powerful.

Then back to her suite to shower and change and eat and study the daily schedule and ready herself for the day ahead. Alexandra was in the communal drawing room lounging and drinking tea as Erin returned from the gym. Alexandra in bare feet and royal blue silk lounge pants and an ivory silk vest. The straps were delicate over Alexandra's own delicate shoulders. Almost pyjamas Erin thought. She had never seen Alexandra like this. She had only seen the perfect public Alexandra. This was the real Alexandra. This Alexandra was without make up, her ashy hair in messy waves, her skin glowing despite the lack of make up. Her eyes still intensely blue, her nipples clearly visible under the ivory silk. Erin felt suddenly deeply uncomfortable, a feeling of desire low in her belly. She couldn't take her eyes off Alexandra.

She stopped still in her sweaty gym kit and looked uncomfortable.

It was Alexandra who spoke,

"Good morning Erin, How was your gym session? You look like you worked hard. Your arms are looking strong." Alexandra's eyes flickered over Erin's biceps and forearms, still wet from exertion.

Erin felt more uncomfortable. Alexandra smiled.

"I have nothing till the dinner with Prince Nicolas of Sweden this evening so I won't be getting ready until later. I am taking a day to relax and stay in."

"Sure, yes. Of course," stammered Erin. "You like Prince Nicolas?" Erin grasped at something to make conversation, then rolled her eyes at herself for the stupidity of her comment.

Alexandra didn't seem phased and smiled curiously.

"Oh, I'm not so sure yet. My father wants me to consider him for marriage. So I guess that is what I am doing. Spending some time with him and considering."

"Oh, erm.... Is that how it works?" Erin asked awkwardly. Still standing near the door in her sweaty clothes. Still staring at Alexandra in loose fitting silk that skimmed her curves.

"Well, sort of. I mean, I get to choose who I marry. But there are, let's say, suggestions. A shortlist of suitable men. The trouble is, I'm not getting any younger, so the pressure to marry is high." Alexandra sighed.

"Wow, I can't imagine having to make that kind of decision," replied Erin.

Alexandra laughed. Something about Erin's awkwardness always tickled her.

"Oh, believe me, I wish I didn't have to. Do you know of Queen Elizabeth the first Erin?"

"Er... sort of. I mean, we did history at school," Erin said vaguely.

"She ruled from 1558 for 44 years. She was a strong female ruler and she never married or produced children despite pressure to do so. I mean, it was a different time. But, I really wish I could do similar."

"Surely you can do as you please? You are Princess Alexandra?" It sounded so simple when Erin said it.

Alexandra laughed.

"Why don't you want to marry?" Erin asked.

Alexandra smiled again, marvelling at this woman who just asked the questions that everyone else avoided.

"Ah, I just wish I had more freedom to choose. Perhaps, if it was the right person. Perhaps, if I was in love, it might feel different. Feel like less of a business arrangement."

"Have you ever been in love?" asked Erin.

"Oh, not really. Once, a long time ago, I kind of thought I was. But it wasn't real. It had no future. These days, perhaps I would have handled things differently." Alexandra looked wistful and there was a sadness in her eyes. "Have you ever been in love Erin?"

Erin blushed, taken aback. "Well, I mean yes. I thought I was. But it turned out she maybe didn't love me so much in return. She turned out to not be that great of a person."

"Maybe we aren't so different after all." Alexandra fixed Erin with her eyes, the blue so intense Erin had to look away first.

"I'd better go get a shower," Erin said. A cold shower, she thought to herself, heat rising between her legs. Heat rising to her face.

Alexandra smiled and nodded and Erin dashed into the safety of her room.

Erin headed straight to the bathroom and turned on the shower while stripping her clothes off. She stepped under the warm water letting it run over her face and down over her body, it felt sensual on her skin. She prayed for the water to wash away her inappropriate thoughts about Alexandra. Alexandra in fine silk, her nipples prominent. Tearing Alexandra out of the fine silk, her nipples in Erin's mouth..... Erin shook her head under the stream of water. This was crazy. This was absolutely crazy.

6

E rin waited in the drawing room and Alexandra emerged at 7pm, exquisite in a long dark red dress with long sleeves that hinted at her body beneath, but remained classy and fitting of her royal stature. Her shimmering hair was pinned up, Alicia had been hard at work. Her face was somehow more beautiful with her hair back from it, the lines of her perfect bone structure catching the light as she moved with effortless grace. Diamonds glinted at her ears and neck. Erin gasped when she saw her.

"You look incredible," the words spilled

out of Erin's mouth before she had time to consider them. She broke the rule that you never speak to the Princess unless she speaks to you first.

Alexandra chose to overlook Erin's mistake and responded.

"Thank you," she replied, genuinely grateful for the compliment. "I wasn't sure if the dress was too much. I've lost a couple of pounds recently after some unflattering photos, so Natalie got this dress in a smaller size than usual. I wasn't sure if I look too, you know, thin?"

Erin looked carefully at her body, a body she had caught herself looking at so many times since starting this job. This was the issue with someone of Alexandra's celebrity. They have to be thinner than the average person. The camera sometimes lies. The cameras of the world cannot be allowed to take a photo where Alexandra looks fat. Fat is something Alexandra cannot afford to be. So Alexandra is thin. Mostly thin. She has a gym, she has a personal trainer, she has a nutritionist and chef. Just thin enough to look perfect in clothes. Just thin enough so her breasts are still full and her ass is still round; she cannot afford to look unfeminine either. Erin could see that if she were naked, Alexandra's ribs and hips would be prominent. Right now, her collarbone was prominent, but her breasts were still full and her waist was still tiny. It was how she needed to be for her job. It was what the people wanted to see.

"You look perfect." Erin responded. "So, so beautiful," she said genuinely.

Alexandra shone in response.

"I won't need you tonight, Erin. The dinner is in the palace. Feel free to take the night off. And please let the other girls and the drivers know to do the same. I won't need anything else tonight."

"Thanks," said Erin. "I'll probably be around. I'm not going anywhere, so if you need anything later…"

Alexandra thanked her and glided out of the room towards the grand hall for dinner with her potential husband, Prince Nicolas.

Erin went back to her room alone.

She couldn't get the image of Alexandra in the red dress out of her mind.

ALEXANDRA SMILED and welcomed everyone to the palace as she sat at the head of the table. She made a special welcome to Prince Nicolas of Sweden, their guest of honour for the evening. He was lean and tall and very gentlemanly with sandy blonde hair. Alexandra contemplated him for a second. Could she imagine him by her side for the rest of her life? Her face screwed up slightly at the thought.

The other nobles, Alexandra knew well. She had known them all for years. Lord Hugo was sitting on one side of her and Prince Nicolas on the other side at the top of the huge table. She still hadn't ended things properly with Hugo. She had kept meaning to, but it just hadn't happened yet. She knew she could never marry him. As she spoke and welcomed everyone, Hugo swilled the dark red wine boldly. This was one of the reasons; every time she saw

Hugo lately he was drinking. Not just socially having a wine, but downing glass after glass, the rich red liquid to his lips as though it was Alexandra's blood he was draining. She felt like that when she was around him lately, uneasy, as though he was going to be angry when she ended things. That was probably why she kept delaying the inevitable. He was always drinking, always seemed volatile. His dark eyes that she had once found charming, she now found accusatory and loose from the alcohol.

"You look very beautiful tonight, Your Royal Highness." Prince Nicolas was charismatic as he took her hand to kiss it and addressed her.

"Why, thank you, kind Prince," responded Alexandra coyly, "Please, call me Alexandra."

"I will, Alexandra, and yourself, please call me Nicolas."

"Too skinny," the unwanted input from the other side. Hugo snapping at her. "Only joking, Your Highness, of course. I just preferred your lovely body before you lost weight."

Alexandra seethed inside but chose not to react. Her body was judged every day of her life, this man that was supposed to want to love her, to care about her, had no right to join in with the scrutiny.

She smiled as though unaffected, "Oh, I guess I had better have a second helping of supper tonight then?"

LATER THAT EVENING, Erin was dozing on her bed fully dressed when she woke to hear raised voices in the drawing room.

"You are an embarrassment Hugo. This sham relationship between us, it cannot go on. Your drinking is worse than ever."

Erin recognised Alexandra's elegant voice instantly.

She recognised Hugo by name. Lord Hugo. According to the newspapers and magazines he was Alexandra's sometime boyfriend and potentially her future husband. She was occasionally photographed with him. Yet, having been in the Princess's service for weeks now, this was the first that Erin had seen of him.

Erin sat up and listened in to what was happening, edging closer to the door, her curiosity ripe.

"For fuck's sake Alexandra, when are we going to take this further? What was this silly play off with that blonde Swedish idiot all about at dinner? You are supposed to be with me. This has been planned our whole lives, that we would grow up and marry. You will never find someone more suitable for the role. You think there are loads of men around that want to live in your shadow? You think it is everyone's ambition to be emasculated like that? Well I'll tell you right now, it isn't. I'm not delighted by the idea, but I have been prepared my whole life to be your husband. I am prepared to give up my own ambition and desires for you. To support you as you become Queen." Lord Hugo's voice was angry and his words were slurred from the alcohol.

"I don't want it, Hugo. I don't want to be with you. This is over between us. This. Us. It is over." Alexandra wanted finality. Erin felt like she was prying into Alexandra's most private moments, but she couldn't help herself. She continued to listen in behind the door.

"Over?" Lord Hugo laughed loudly. "How can something be over when it never actually begun? We have been together 5 years Alexandra. For the cameras. You kiss me for the cameras, you hold my hand for the cameras. In private, nothing. You won't even spend your evening with me if you can help it. You need to lighten up. You need to actually try it. You aren't seventeen anymore, this virgin crap is wearing terribly thin."

Erin heard commotion and a bang and something fall and smash on the tiled floor. She heard Alexandra gasp.

"Get off me. Get your hands off me." Alexandra's voice sounded panicked.

There was a split second when Erin had to choose whether to burst out and interrupt them or not. Was this her job? Or would Alexandra consider it interfering in her personal life?

She waited.

She heard Alexandra gasp and cry out and there was more commotion. Erin burst out of her door into the hallway. She saw

Lord Hugo pinning Alexandra against the wall, his big figure blocking her exit, his left hand tightly gripping Alexandra's wrists. The weight of him pinned her back. The skirt of her long red dress was pushed up around her hips and his right hand was ferreting underneath, pushing between her legs.

He turned his head when he heard Erin's entrance and he laughed.

"Get the fuck out of here, this is between the Princess and myself." Hugo's voice was loud and intimidating. Erin imagined his hot sour breath on Alexandra's beautiful face.

"Call your fucking dog off, Ally." Hugo spat at Alexandra.

Her eyes looked to Erin, fear and desperation in them.

"You heard the Princess. Get your hands off her," said Erin more confidently than she felt. Lord Hugo was a powerful man who didn't want to be told 'no'.

"She is my fucking girlfriend. I'll do what I like. What are you going to do about it? Shoot me? I always said having a stupid little girl playing as a bodyguard was a dumb idea, but you wouldn't listen Ally, would you?"

In seconds, Erin responded. She wrenched his right arm away from the Princess, taking him momentarily off balance and then pulled it into a painful hold up behind his back. Hugo shouted and let go of Alexandra who collapsed to the floor.

Erin had complete control over him now, as he moved to resist she just lifted the arm lock slightly and he yelped in pain.

She walked him to the door of Alexandra's suite of rooms and said to him, "If you get out of here right now, I won't call the rest of the security team. Never ever treat any woman like that. Never ever treat the Princess like that again." Erin tightened her hold, causing him intense pain. "Do you agree to leave quietly if I release you?"

"For fuck's sake. Yes, whatever. Just let go of my fucking arm. I'll have you done for assault." Hugo stammered in shock.

Erin let go of him and opened the door. Her eyes, aggressive and threatening as she used her body and the door to usher him out, closing and locking the door quickly behind him.

Erin looked to the Princess, crumpled on the floor.

"Do you want me to call further security for him? Do you want me to report this?" she asked gently.

"No, no, please don't," said Alexandra, tears on her fine cheekbones.

Erin knelt next to the Princess kindly, she looked so small and fragile suddenly, huddled on the floor, her beautiful dress torn and her makeup smudged. "Can I call anyone for you?"

Alexandra looked up, her blue eyes big and scared. "Please, no. I don't want anyone to know."

"Let me help you to your room." Erin offered her hand and the Princess took it. Erin stood strong and pulled Alexandra up from the floor.

Alexandra clung to Erin's arm, her perfume strong in the silence. Erin guided her to her bedroom, the rooms that were so busy during the day, empty now at night after her staff had been sent home. Erin was the only one who lived so close. It was the first time she had seen inside Alexandra's bedroom and Erin was blown away by the splendour. Erin had never seen a four poster bed before, but here one was in this huge room. Rich dark hand carved wood, with white veils and curtains all around it. A canopy of white for the Princess. A hint of contemporary amongst the traditional and the antique. The old amongst the new. The Princess with her bodyguard.

Alexandra sat on the edge of her bed, looking shell shocked.

She looked up at Erin again. "Erin, please stay with me. Please help me."

Erin had never seen anyone more delicate and vulnerable than the wide eyed Princess before her.

"Of course Ma'am. Whatever you need." Erin said. "Shall I run you a bath?" Erin asked.

Alexandra didn't really reply, so Erin went ahead to the huge bathroom suite and the vast bath and turned on the taps anyway. She found some luxury bath creme that claimed to be Amber and Vanilla. It smelt beautiful so she added it to the hot water, its shimmery pale gold liquid swirling and dispersing under and into the water.

She returned to the bedroom with a white towelling robe and Alexandra was still sitting there, almost catatonic. Erin picked up her hand and asked if she wanted to take the dress and jewellery off.

She nodded but made no attempt to remove anything.

"Shall I help you?" Erin asked, so cautious of overstepping boundaries, but at the same time, so keen to help this troubled woman.

Alexandra nodded again. Erin began by gently unclasping her necklace. She was surprised at the weight of the diamonds as she lifted it from Alexandra's collarbone. She removed the diamonds from her ears and lifted her hand to remove her bracelet. As she unclasped the bracelet she saw the skin beginning to form shades of blue and purple around her slim wrist.

Erin asked if it was ok to help her off with her dress. Another despondent nod. Erin slid it from her shoulders and helped her pull her arms through, as though helping a child undress. She wore no bra. Her breasts were surprisingly full against her prominent ribs and narrow shoulders. Erin helped her stand and slipped the torn dress down over her hips and it fell in a pile on the floor.

Princess Alexandra stood before her in small white panties, there were more bruises beginning to appear on her arms; Erin immediately helped her on with the soft robe. She wrapped Alexandra up in it, it was way too big for her. Erin's desire for this woman momentarily overcome with her desire to care for her. Alexandra slipped off her own underwear and sat back on the bed and looked vacant.

"Ma'am, are you ok? Should I call someone? The palace doctor? I think maybe I should?" Erin was scared suddenly. Scared that this wasn't something she should be dealing with alone.

"Please, no, Erin. Please no. I don't want anyone to know." Alexandra re-iterated. "Please call me Alexandra."

And suddenly they were just two women with a secret. Erin and Alexandra. Alexandra needed her help.

Erin sat beside her and removed the pins from her hair, one by one, tenderly, letting the ashy waves fall piece by piece around her shoulders.

It felt like there was a trust between them, a deepening of their relationship suddenly. To something more.

Erin checked the bath and turned off the taps.

"Alexandra, the bath is ready." It felt strange calling her Alexandra. Strange, but somehow right.

"Will you sit with me? I don't want to be alone," Alexandra asked as she dropped her robe, walked to the bath and stepped into the steaming bubbles.

Erin was star stuck for a second as she watched her, Princess Alexandra, naked and ethereal. People didn't say no to the future Queen. She knew that. Of course Erin would sit with her.

There was a stool in the big bathroom that Erin sat on, positioning herself so as to avert her eyes from the Princess's body under the water.

"I can't believe he did that." Alexandra broke the silence.

"Has he ever done anything like that before?" Erin queried.

"God, no. I mean, when I have been alone with him and he has been drinking, he can get a bit pushy. But I've known him all my life. At one time I thought I would marry him. I guess it is my own fault. I led him on too much. He has actually been very patient with me. I should have just let him have sex with me already." Alexandra hung her head.

"Alexandra, NO. Absolutely not. You should never have sex with someone because you feel like you should. This was not your fault. He was a brute. A vile pig. Nobody should ever behave like that. Your body is not his property. I'm so sorry, I should have acted sooner. I just didn't know for sure what to do. I didn't want to interfere. I wasn't sure what you wanted." Erin felt angry at the man who had hurt her. Erin felt angry at the world that made this incredible woman believe that something like this could possibly be her fault.

"Erin, I cannot thank you enough for being there and for what you did. If you hadn't been there it would have been so much worse, I'm sure. He wouldn't have stopped. I couldn't have stopped him. He is so much bigger than me."

"Of course," Erin replied. "That is what I am here for. I will always protect you. I just wish I could have done more. I wish I could have intervened earlier. Before it went that far."

There was a gentle peace between them as Alexandra washed herself and Erin sat quietly next to her, the scent of amber and vanilla heavy in the air. The whole experience was surreal, but Erin found her heart full with love for the Princess. She wanted so fiercely to protect her and care for her, but evil had come for her, from where it was least expected. Erin knew she had to be better at her job, but at the same time feared for what might happen if Lord Hugo accused her of assault. Hopefully it would never come to that.

Back in Alexandra's bedroom, wrapped tightly in her fluffy robe, Alexandra said, "Erin, will you hold me? Please?"

Their eyes met and it seemed on one level like the most natural thing in the world and on another level deeply inappropriate. Erin agreed to and opened her arms and Alexandra folded into them like a troubled child, her face to Erin's breast, her hair damp through Erin's shirt.

They stayed like that for a while, Erin stroked her face and her hair. Alexandra cried. Day to day, this woman was so tightly wound. Day to day, she could never let anything out like this. Erin gave her strong arms in which to collapse into.

Erin kissed the top of her head, before she had even thought about what she was doing. Alexandra didn't move. Maybe she hadn't noticed. Maybe, they could both pretend that hadn't happened. Probably best if they both pretended none of this had happened.

Alexandra fell asleep in Erin's arms eventually and Erin gently and quietly tried to extract herself and leave Alexandra on the bed without waking her. She found a big blanket and put it over her sleeping form.

For a moment she looked at the Princess's troubled face in the hazy light from the lamp. Her eyelashes flickered lightly as she dreamed.

Then she pulled herself together, remembered who this woman was and who she herself was, and she turned and walked away.

In the world we live in, that kind of love does not exist.

7

The following morning all was quiet as Erin attended the 7am security briefing, her personal training and the gym. Nobody had a clue what had happened the night before, and she wasn't about to tell them. She headed back up to Alexandra's suite to find it a hive of activity. All of the girls preparing Alexandra for her day of public engagements. Everything was going ahead as usual. Alexandra was disturbingly normal and there was no sign of the vulnerable girl from the night before.

"Morning Erin." Alexandra's lovely voice was as normal and warm as ever as she sat patiently in hair and make up as Alicia worked away at her, her face deep in concentration.

"Morning Ma'am," Erin was back to the professional. Back to work. Forgetting what she had seen last night, the Princess's stunning naked body still etched in her mind.

"Morning Erin," called Jess, busying around everyone. "Be ready for 11am departure, you have the schedule, yes?"

"Yes, got it, thanks Jess. I'll be ready."

And that was it. Back to another day as the Princess's bodyguard. As though nothing had ever happened. Alexandra was troubling with the ease at which she slipped into her public persona. She was so talented at being the Princess that everyone wanted to see.

Erin noticed that she wore a light cashmere sweater with very long sleeves that almost extended onto her hands. She wondered if Alexandra had mentioned her bruises to Natalie and if so, how she had explained them away. It felt like the truth was too much. Too much for Alexandra, too much for a Princess. Too much for her adoring public. Telling one person would mean that person telling one or two others and those people the same. People couldn't resist sharing stories of royalty, rumours of celebrity, nuggets of personal information about those who are like us but different. Those who are born to higher things. The journalists wait like vultures. They love Alexandra, and the opportunity to publish Alexandra as the 'almost-rape-victim' with the perpetrator her 'boyfriend', Lord Hugo, would be the fleshiest corpse for them to feast on. Alexandra was fiercely private and clearly didn't want that story in the papers. Her relationship with Lord Hugo had been closely guarded throughout although Erin was shocked to hear that they had never had sex. She wasn't sure how it worked for royalty, but surely they were allowed to have sex before marriage? Surely they didn't all sit around virginal, waiting to only have sex for procreation of future heirs?

Erin wondered for a moment why Alexandra had trusted her. Because she had. There had been no desperate 'Please don't tell anyone.' this morning. There had just been normality and moving on. Dealing with things perhaps the only way

Alexandra knew how. Over the weeks Erin had spent in the palace, it had become painfully clear that there was nobody Alexandra was really close to. It was obvious watching her life, how guarded she really was.

They headed out later that morning to a Charity lunch for one of the children's charities that Alexandra supported. She looked thoughtful and distant in the back of the black Range Rover as they drove. Her driver was cheery and she said a happy 'Good Morning' to him and asked about his children, then she went back to mute. Erin remembered the rules fine today and didn't create conversation. It was a long drive in silence.

The Range Rover pulled up at the Berkeley hotel. Erin jumped out, there were paparazzi there already and after a quick scan and the nod from the Security who were already there, she opened the door for Alexandra. The Princess stepped out, as graceful as ever, walking in heels as if she had never worn anything else. She smiled, brighter than the sunshine and posed for photographs, lovely, genial, everything the people wanted to see.

Erin escorted her through the huge entrance hall, beautiful marble flooring and columns surrounding them, they walked straight through to the ballroom where the event was being held. Alexandra's public self was shining, her patience endless as she shook hands with person after person, asking them about their lives, focussing on them for those few minutes, fixing them with her intense eyes, making them feel like the only person in the world.

Erin liked to watch her work at events like this. The Princess was truly gifted. Or perhaps had honed this craft just through a lifetime of practice. How much of it was the real her? Erin wondered if Alexandra even knew what was real any more.

The lunch passed, the Princess spoke in front of everyone, her every word captivating. After the lunch, her people still wanted more of her. A little more. A little touch from Royalty. A photo with her perhaps. Or another conversation. They wanted to touch her hand. They wanted anything they could get from her.

The day passed without incident and Alexandra retired to bed early in the evening and dismissed the staff.

Erin wished she could go to Alexandra. To care for her; to love her. But it wasn't an option. She couldn't just go round and see how Alexandra was. It was as if their intimacy from the night before had just been silently erased when they fell asleep.

Erin lay on her bed restless and her phone rang, it was her mother. She toyed with the idea of ignoring it again, but decided against it. She swiped to accept the call.

"Erin! Where have you been? I've been worried sick! I've not heard from you for weeks! I called you so many times. I even texted you!"

"Mum, I told you, I'm working for the Princess. It is full on. I can't just answer my phone whenever I feel like it. This is a very important job, you know."

"Oh yes honey, of course. I have told all my friends about it. Did you see that photo of you with her in the Daily Mail the other day? Faint and in the background, you are, but it is definitely you. It would be better if you could stand right next to her next time you see cameras then you can get right there in the photo."

Erin sighed.

"So, what's she really like? This Princess Alexandra? She always seems so wonderful. Our country is very lucky to have someone like her leading the way," her mum asked.

"Oh, erm, yes. She is lovely. Wonderful. Very kind to everyone she meets." Erin responded.

"Oh, that's brilliant darling. I can't wait to tell your father."

Erin's mother launched in to tell Erin everything that had happened in her own life recently without Erin asking. Erin left the phone on the bed while she went to clean her teeth and when she picked it back up, her mother was still talking.

The phone call lasted an hour. Erin managed to tolerate it, purely as a distraction from thinking about Alexandra, from wanting so desperately to go to her and see if she was okay. She couldn't do that.

Erin found herself distancing herself more and more from her own life and immersing herself in her role as Alexandra's shadow. There wasn't a huge amount to lose from her own life. She felt better with less contact with her family. Sophie would text sometimes and Erin just wouldn't respond. She had no interest anymore. None at all.

Alexandra was her life now.

8

The next morning, early horse riding was scheduled, so immediately after the security team briefing, they headed out to the country estate where the horses were stabled. Erin wasn't sure she was strictly needed on horseback for this as technically the cars could follow at a distance round the estate, so she asked Alexandra.

"No cars, Alexandra said to the team. I'll just have Sergeant Kennedy with me on a horse. Keep everyone else as far away from me as possible."

The crisp early morning frost clung to each blade of grass and the calm was loud in it's silence. Erin and Alexandra mounted their horses. Alexandra's lovely face was pensive so Erin kept a respectful distance and resisted making any conversation. The horses walked quietly through the cold, their hooves the only sound. Fog hung on the air where their breath was.

After twenty minutes, Alexandra began to talk.

"I like this, you know. It is my favourite time. Out here, in the morning, with the horses."

"You don't mind the cold?" Erin asked.

"No, not at all," replied Alexandra. "When I was a child, I would come to the stables and ride at every opportunity. I wish I had the chance more often as an adult, but, well, you've seen my schedule. I have a pretty busy life. A lot of commitments."

"Hugo was apologetic the next morning," Alexandra continued. "Of course he was. He could have been in so much trouble for what he did."

Erin was surprised to hear Alexandra bring it up.

"What will come of it?" Erin asked, curious.

"Nothing," said Alexandra. "I will never tell anyone, and I would appreciate it if you could keep the same discretion. I will never speak to him ever again. His loss is greater, you see. He potentially could have married the future Queen, but now, he never will."

"You think you actually would have married him? Lord Hugo? Even before all of this?" Erin asked.

Alexandra sighed a deep and world weary sigh. "Oh, perhaps not. I was with him because the public needed something to see. The press needed something to photograph and write about. There was never anything real there."

"You said before you had sort of been in love with someone before? Or you thought you were at least? Why couldn't you marry him?" Erin asked.

There was a moment of silence as Alexandra thought carefully about her answer.

"Her." she corrected.

The word released so easily from her lips had a world of weight attached to it. The word settled in the air.

Her.

Her.

Her.

It suddenly made sense to Erin why Alexandra was so guarded. Why she didn't want to have sex with Lord Hugo. Why she was so reluctant to marry.

"Oh... well I wasn't expecting that response!" Erin laughed and it broke the ice in the air. Alexandra laughed too, more cautiously.

"So, who was she? What happened?" Erin waited for Alexandra to tell her to mind her own business or to never tell anyone else. But she didn't, the trust was there between them now.

"I've never spoken about this before." Alexandra waited a moment and then spoke. "She was my friend, it was years ago. We had a secret fling for a while, I guess you would say. I had feelings for her. I thought I loved her. She ended up finishing things with me to marry a Lord. She told me there would never be a world that would allow either of us to be with a woman. That the world itself might have progressed, but not our world. Not the world of Royalty. That there would never be a day where it would be accepted for a member of the Royal family to come out as gay. And, as much as I hate it and have hated it ever since, she was right. I've looked at it from all angles. From every way there is to look at it. The trouble is, I'm not just a fringe player in the family. I am the heir to the throne. It is different for me; it always has been. There is no way out, I will have to get married to a man, sooner or later and I will have to bear children."

Alexandra was so nobly resigned to her fate.

"What happened to her? Are you still friends?" Erin asked.

"Oh, she is married now. She has three children. Yes I still see her very occasionally. We have never spoken since about what happened between us. I doubt we ever will. I don't think her feelings were as strong as mine."

"I don't think anything you did would ever change the way the public see you, you know?" Erin said. "Everyone, without exception, adores you. If anyone could change things for the future of the monarchy, you could."

Alexandra smiled wryly. "Unfortunately, I don't think it will work quite like that. Also, there's not exactly a long list of eligible lesbians for Princesses to date!"

"I think you would find that if you came out, there suddenly would be a list a mile long of women who wanted to go gay for Princess Alexandra."

Alexandra laughed. "Thanks for your vote of confidence. Come on, I'm getting cold. Let's warm things up." She squeezed her horse forward into a trot.

Just like that, the conversation was over and Erin held the biggest secret in the world in her hands.

9

The following afternoon, Erin accompanied the Princess and Prince Nicolas of Sweden on a walk around Hyde Park. It was relatively unscheduled which gave them a certain amount of freedom. They wore sunglasses and Alexandra wasn't immediately recognised and the Prince wasn't a well known face in the UK. Erin was in the curious situation of gatecrashing their date. She followed at a suitable distance, keen to get to know Prince Nicolas, keen to make her own mind up if he was any good for Alexandra.

Nicolas was tall and nice enough. But bland. Nicolas was bland. This was quickly

very obvious. Could Alexandra really re-
duce herself to this? How quickly would
her sharp mind dull when she married a
man like Prince Nicolas? How would she
manage to hide her true self for the rest of
their lives together? How would she find a
way to lie down and open her legs for him?
Women had before, of course. For the
whole of time itself, women had been
opening their legs for men they didn't love,
didn't want, men that repulsed them.
Women had forced themselves to endure
sex they didn't want enough times, perhaps
Alexandra finding a way to force herself
through sex with a man like Prince Nicolas
would be nothing new.

The very thought of it made Erin sad.
She saw how upset Alexandra had been
after the unwanted advances of Lord Hugo.
Would Alexandra be able to find a way to
distance herself enough to have sex with a
man she didn't want? Alexandra had confided in her about her problems. By the
sounds of it, Erin was the only person that
Alexandra had confided in. Surely she
should have given Alexandra some advice?
But, what advice was there?

Don't marry someone you don't love.

That would be good advice. But advice for someone in Alexandra's position, really wasn't quite that straightforward.

No wonder Alexandra was so guarded. She was guarding the biggest secret someone of her fame could ever guard. Nobody had any idea.

They went for dinner at Nobu and then later in the evening, back at the palace Prince Nicolas went back to Alexandra's suite with her and Alexandra dismissed the staff. Erin went to her room feeling something was really wrong. She went to her bathroom and vomited. She was jealous. Angry and jealous. Sick with the thought that Nicolas might touch Alexandra. That he might touch the body that Erin had loved and cared for when Alexandra was hurt.

As Erin sat quietly in her room, straining to hear anything through the walls, she knew for sure what she had been suspecting for a while. She was falling in love with Princess Alexandra.

It was late when Erin heard the Prince

leave. She wanted again to go and check on Alexandra, but she couldn't. It wasn't the way things worked. She lay restlessly in bed.

In the room across the hall, on the four poster bed draped in white, Alexandra lay restlessly too. What was she doing? What did she want?

10

The rest of the week passed uneventfully. Prince Nicolas headed back to Sweden and Erin and Alexandra slipped back into their day to day. Conversations remained professional. Alexandra remained guarded.

On Saturday night Alexandra sent the staff home early and text Erin asking her to join her in her drawing room.

Erin was confused, yet curious. What did Alexandra want? She slipped her jeans on and knocked on the door of the drawing room.

"Come in, have a seat." Alexandra's

voice silky and seductive. At least, it was in Erin's head.

Erin entered and sat down.

"Erin, thank you for joining me. I have a special request tonight. It needs to be very very discreet. I cannot have any of the rest of the security team knowing. I cannot have anyone knowing. It will be a secret mission, if you like."

Erin looked to her curiously.

"I want to go to Soho. To a gay bar. Just you and me. No other security."

"What?!" Erin was shocked. "No way," she said. "I mean, no way, ma'am. It isn't possible. It isn't safe. You would be recognised."

"I have a plan," responded Alexandra emptying an overnight bag onto the antique table. As she spread out the items, Erin saw a long brown wig, some coloured contact lenses, some skinny jeans, a cool vest top, some converse trainers. Had Alexandra gone completely mad?!

"Ma'am, please. I don't think you understand. It could be very dangerous." Erin had so many concerns about this plan. Everything about it was risky. Everything about it went against all security protocol. She would lose her job if anyone found out.

"It will work Erin, I promise." As she spoke she pulled the wig on over her own hair, long and wavy dark chocolate. She had a small mirror on the table and she used it to apply the dark brown contact lenses. Her eyes immediately looked so different. Erin barely recognised her. She stripped down to her underwear in the middle of the room, black lace tempting Erin momentarily, before she pulled on the tight black jeans and the white rock-chick vest.

As Erin looked at her, she thought perhaps she was right. Nobody surely would recognise her. So much of her public identity was her expensive looking ashy hair and her wide blue eyes. The way she dressed. And her persona.

All of that was gone suddenly. A very different version of Alexandra was there behind the contact lenses. Her personality seemed different, full of fun, intrigue and excitement. The dark eyes sparkled with desire.

"Please Erin, please. Take me out. I

want to be free. I've used disguises before, it does work. I just never ever get opportunity to walk freely in this world. I want that. Just for tonight, please. Take me to your world."

She was clearly having some kind of mid life crisis.

Erin was torn between knowing that she absolutely shouldn't agree to this. But at the same time, knowing that she would agree to it. That you just didn't say no to Alexandra.

Alexandra looked striking in her new look, but surprisingly small without heels on.

"What if they ask you for ID?" Erin asked.

Alexandra reached inside the bag and pulled out a fake ID. Her fake picture and a fake name.

Isobel Andrews

"Well, hello Ms Isobel. You really have thought of everything." Erin laughed.

"You can call me Izzy," she responded, different in how she held herself, different in how she spoke.

"Here." She reached back into the bag and threw a top and a butter-soft black leather biker jacket to Erin. I thought maybe you wouldn't have packed for this eventuality. I got you these. She smiled. "I thought they would suit you. Put them on," she requested. Or commanded. It wasn't really a request.

Erin, less confident than Alexandra, undid her shirt and took it off cautiously, placing it down. She stood in her sports bra, feeling self conscious as she hurried to put on the clothes from Alexandra.

"Oh, you look amazing! I just knew that jacket would suit you!" Alexandra lit up with excitement. I know you don't really wear make up, but please let me do make up for you?"

Erin succumbed to the make up; a live doll for Alexandra to play with. Alexandra's fingers in her hair, her face inches from Erin's own as she concentrated on doing make up. An hour later, Alexandra had made them both up and straightened Erin's hair. Erin barely recognised herself with heavy kohl liner round her eyes. Alexandra had some hair and make up skills that were wasted on a Princess. She finished and was proud of her work. Erin looked at them both together in the mirror, they looked like rock stars.

"Give me one compromise, please wear your GPS wristband. You don't have to turn it on unless anything happens, but I just need a backup plan." It was a terrible back up plan, as far as security of such a high profile individual goes, everything about the plan for the night was risky as hell, but Alexandra seemed to be enjoying it, she seemed more alive than Erin had ever seen her and Erin couldn't help just wanting to please her.

"Ok, if you insist." Alexandra's dark eyes flashed.

The next step was to smuggle her out of the palace and grounds. Alexandra produced the keys to one of her own Range Rovers. She rarely drove herself, but she was perfectly capable of driving. Erin headed out of their rooms onto the communal corridor to take a look around. It was 8pm, all was quiet. She went back for Alexandra and they both hurried to the fire exit where they could get outside quickly.

They got out to the garages without being caught. They were like naughty schoolchildren as they ran to Alexandra's Range Rover which she had made sure had been left out ready for her.

"I think once we are out of the palace grounds we should get a taxi." Erin said. "To turn up in a taxi will be the most discreet way. We don't want to be seen getting out of a vehicle like this."

They drove towards security on the palace gates. The good news is it is easier to get out of the palace than to get in. They pulled up towards the barrier and Alexandra raised a hand to the guard and smiled. God only knows who he thought was in that Range Rover but he raised the barrier and let them out. They were free in the city for the night. Erin felt exposed without any form of back up. She had worn her weapon underneath her leather jacket, just in case, the polymer body of her Glock cold against her skin. Alexandra was buoyed with confidence in Erin, but Erin knew that no bodyguard is effective alone. No bodyguard works alone without even a driver. She would be foolish to think she could offer any reasonable protection. If she had to defend them, she was limited as to what she could do.

They parked a few streets away and walked on the street together as they waited for a taxi.

"I'm excited Erin. I feel so free." Alexandra smiled as they walked. "Thank you so much for this. It is the greatest gift anyone could give me. I haven't been anywhere without security in my whole life. Well, I'm not without security, I have you. But, I feel so free. Thank you."

"You are welcome! I hope Soho lives up to your hopes!" Erin waved down a black London cab and it pulled over for them, they got in the back and sat next to each other. Alexandra's slim thighs in black denim, so close to Erin's own thighs. Erin's thighs longer and so much more muscular than Alexandra's. It began to feel like a date. A night out. Not like work. Erin's mind flew between desire for Alexandra and desire to keep her safe. Scanning for danger, scanning her body and her face.

They pulled up in Soho, the heart of the London underbelly, and as they stepped out onto the street Alexandra stood mesmerised, taking it all in. The hustle of the people on the streets, pavements busy with tables and chairs, with front of house staff trying to draw people in to their businesses. Erin knew their biggest risk was not so much being recognised, but being pickpocketed or mugged. She walked glued close to Alexandra, ready to defend her at any moment. Alexandra wandered aimlessly.

"This place is amazing Erin. There is such a life to it. Such a heartbeat. Can we go in this bar?" Alexandra took her arm and dragged her into the first bar with a rainbow flag hanging proudly outside of it.

Saturday night was busy and suddenly the people up close pressed in the busy bar seemed to surprise Alexandra.

Erin took the lead, took her hand, felt it warm in her own and lead Alexandra to an upstairs bar. It was quieter. There was a balcony overlooking the downstairs area. Alexandra was like a child in a sweet shop, watching everything as though in a trance.

"Can I have a cocktail here?" Alexandra asked.

"Sure," replied Erin. "It might not be as good as you are used to though."

"Surprise me."

Alexandra pushed a bundle of immaculately pressed bank notes into Erin's hand.

"Please use this to pay for everything tonight."

Erin wanted to argue. Her pride wanted to argue, but she didn't. She took the money and went to the bar. No further than five feet from Alexandra and with one eye on her the whole time.

She returned with cocktails for them both. She made sure her own was non alcoholic. Alexandra was delighted with the sweet taste on her tongue. Her face lit up as Erin handed the vibrant red drink to her. Erin couldn't help noticing Alexandra's lips tight around the straw.

"I can't believe I am actually in Soho. It's like the heart of the London gay scene right?" asked Alexandra.

Erin smiled at her childlike enthusiasm. "Sure is!" responded Erin.

"Do you come here often?" asked Alexandra.

Erin laughed. "Is that a chat up line?"

Alexandra laughed, her eyes bright behind the contact lenses.

"I mean, I literally just meant, you must come here all the time. It is such a magical place." She sipped her cocktail thoughtfully.

Erin had never thought of Soho as magical. When she had been here with her friends, fun nights often ended in dirty kebabs and staggering around trying to find the night bus home. Looking at Soho through Alexandra's eyes was refreshing. She felt the risqué vibe of the streets. She felt the beating heart of the small village nestled inside a big city.

"Not so much, I mean now and again, but I'm no party animal."

Alexandra finished her cocktail and grabbed Erin's arm dragging her down the stairs and out of the bar.

She walked ahead of Erin along the street, fascinated by everything.

"A tattoo shop. I had no idea late night tattoos was a thing! I could get one!" The princess was dangerous in her excitement.

"Wow! Er, no.. You definitely can't! Can you imagine if anyone found out?"

Alexandra's face was up close to the tattoo shop window as she saw a woman inside getting tattooed. She opened the door and went in.

"Excuse me, I was just wondering if you would mind if we watched?"

The tattooist, a big guy in his 40s, his bald head covered in tattoos, barely looked up. "If the lady doesn't mind," he grunted.

The 'lady' was more of a girl and looked barely old enough to be out without an adult accompanying her. "Sure, I don't mind."

The girl was leaning forwards on a purpose built chair, her whole back exposed as he worked on an intricate Tiger on her back. Erin watched Alexandra's eyes as they followed every movement. His tattoo machine, it's tiny needles, dipped in the ink pots and then onto her skin. Into her skin. Marking her indelibly for life. A cloth in his other hand wiping away excess ink and revealing the art he was creating.

It was such an intimate procedure to watch. Alexandra was fixated, and Erin found herself mesmerised too. Sitting in this seedy tattoo shop watching the artist at work. And he was a true artist. Erin had perhaps never really appreciated what tattooing involved. She felt like she was seeing the world through new eyes seeing everything alongside Alexandra, as though for the first time. Erin forgot for a moment, who she was there with, what her role was. It felt like the most natural thing in the world to be sitting there with this woman, safe in the cocoon of bright lights in this tiny shop. The buzzing of the needles in the tattoo machine, a rhythmic hum.

Alexandra's no doubt expensive wig was so convincing. The long dark hair looking like part of her. Her eyes, heavily lined in black liner were curiously dark and unnatural in appearance in the bright lights. The one thing for sure is she looked absolutely nothing like the Princess that the people knew and loved.

Minutes passed as they sat there. Next to each other. Curiously close.

Then Alexandra prepared to leave. She left a couple of £20 notes on the side as they left.

"Thank you so much for letting us join you. Your Tiger is beautiful."

There was little response and no break in the work as Alexandra and Erin were back in the hustle of the street.

"I have never seen so many lesbians." Alexandra said as they walked.

"How do you know they are lesbians?" Erin challenged.

Alexandra smiled. "Yes, you are right. I shouldn't judge. Nobody ever really knows by looking. But they are just so cool. Their haircuts, their clothes, their tattoos and piercings. I feel so plain. They look so exotic."

"I assure you, they probably aren't that exotic," Erin laughed, "and you are anything but plain."

Out in the street, Alexandra spotted a sex shop and ran across the road to it. It's neon sign literally drawing her in like a moth to a flame.

A wide eyed Alexandra, "I have literally always wanted to go in one of these shops. Can we go in? Please?"

Erin reasoned that they were probably much safer in places although there was a somewhat questionable security guard on the door. They headed down the stairs into the basement shop and Erin laughed as Alexandra picked up a huge black dildo. "What on earth is this? Surely it is too big for anyone?"

"I mean, I think this range is targeted at gay men. How about this one?" Erin picked up another of the big black toys, this one in the shape of an arm and fist.

"Oh my god. Let me see it." Alexandra took it and weighed it in her hand. "I just can't believe it."

Erin picked up another dildo, a carefully carved nun or something similar. They both just laughed.

"Surely not," said Alexandra.

"Oh, this is just the tip of the iceberg." Erin knew damn well what the shop was likely to contain and she found herself enjoying experiencing it all with Alexandra.

THEY HEADED to a couple more bars and the evening got busier. The princess was wide eyed throughout and somehow completely anonymous. Even Erin would have struggled to recognise her if she hadn't known.

They went to a crowded girls only bar. It was underground and dimly lit. A fit dancer in her underwear danced on a pole. Erin found herself pushed close to Alexandra, there just wasn't enough space for anything else. Her heart raced and the atmosphere between them felt electric. Alexandra brushed against her and Erin felt it everywhere.

"Let's dance." Alexandra took her hand and pulled her into the dancefloor. Erin had never been much of a dancer but found herself swept away with Alexandra's enthusiasm. The deep pulse of the music took them to another world. Alexandra's strangely dark eyes promised another world.

A tall woman with a too cool haircut danced closely behind Alexandra, her eyes predatory up and down Alexandra's body. Alexandra danced with her, her eyes slightly unsure but enjoying the attention until the tall woman put her hands on Alexandras hips and pulled her in. Alexandra about jumped out of her skin. Not used to the unwanted attentions of strangers. Alexandra was clearly horrified that this touching without consent was something that happened in clubs. Her eyes looked momentarily panicked and sought the safety of Erin.

"She's with me," Erin said confidently and with an air of ownership and pulled Alexandra back towards her.

The tall woman put her hands up and accepted defeat easily.

"Sorry, mate." Erin saw her mouth an apology.

Safe enough so far, thought Erin.

Alexandra clung to Erin for a few seconds too long. She clung to the safety of Erin and everything that Erin was to her. Without her usual heels on, the top of her dark wig reached Erin's chin. She felt the Princess's face close against her breast, just for that moment and it was overwhelming.

They pulled apart and danced again to the music. Alexandra staying closer this time and avoiding eye contact with other women. The intensity building between them was not lost on either woman.

As they left the bar and went back out to the street where they could hear each other again, Alexandra enthused about the bar.

"What an incredible place. I've never been anywhere like that. All those women. All those women just like us. Do they normally just touch people like that? Is that a normal thing?"

"Pretty normal, yeah," Erin sighed. "It is a bar on a Saturday night. People drinking and dancing. These things just happen really. It doesn't make it okay, but it happens a lot. At least she backed away when I stepped in."

Alexandra looked to her and took in Erin's height and strong shoulders. Their eyes met.

"Thank you for saving me."

"Anytime," replied Erin, not realising how soon her words might be tested.

11

E rin and Alexandra headed out of Soho's hustle trying to find a taxi that was available. It was a busy night and black cabs drove past but they were already occupied.

A lone drunk man approached them, his gait slightly wobbly, his voice slightly slurred.

"Lesbians," he proclaimed. "Are you two lesbians?"

"Ignore him and keep walking." Erin directed Alexandra as they kept moving.

"I love lesbians," he continued as he turned and walked with them. "Especially ones that look like you two. I like her. The little dark one. What is your name?"

Erin was on edge and suddenly felt very exposed. Suddenly very aware she had no back up. The man was old enough to know better, old enough to behave like an adult, but it was amazing how often straight men behaved like this when they saw lesbians.

"How do lesbians have sex? Really though? It is a serious question... stop ignoring me."

Alexandra started to look concerned as Erin increased their pace. He increased his pace to keep with them.

"Seriously though. Which one of you is the man? It's you isn't it? You, the tall one. I bet you wear the strap on. Does little darkie like it or does she want a real man?"

"Listen to me!!" he shouted as they neared a main road.

Suddenly he lurched and lunged towards Alexandra grabbing at her body. He caught her hair and her wig came off in his hands. He looked surprised and grabbed again for her. Erin responded swiftly and brutally. The heel of her hand smashed straight into his nose and he screamed as the impact hit him. Angered, he let go of Alexandra and turned on Erin swinging his fist towards her. She blocked his flailing arm and struck him swiftly with her elbow and then followed it with her knee sharply up into his groin. He crumpled to the ground immediately wailing in pain and bloodied all over his face. People started to come out of the nearest bar to see what was happening. A car pulled over. Erin grabbed Alexandra who was standing stupefied.

"Run."

Alexandra didn't move.

"RUN." Erin grabbed her hand and pulled her. She knew there was no way they could be caught there. Anyone coming too close now would recognise Alexandra for sure without the wig on. They ran down the streets into the rabbit warren of Soho rounding corners as fast as Erin could drag her, then into a dark alleyway and a shop doorway. Adrenaline coursed through them both as Erin slammed the Princess into the doorway to hide for a second. To catch their breath; to make a plan.

And suddenly Alexandra was pushed against the wall and Erin was so close to her and her breath was ragged. Erin's eyes were on high alert and her heart was beating out of her chest. Alexandra took hold of Erin's leather jacket and pulled Erin's strong body in towards her.

Erin paused, shocked for a second as Alexandra looked up to her inches from her face.

"Kiss me," she said breathily. Erin paused again looking at Alexandra's beautiful face, the curiously dark eyes flooded with desire and her own ashy hair slicked back. Her collarbone prominent in the dark.

"Kiss me," repeated Alexandra and Erin couldn't fight her own lust any longer. She pushed Alexandra back against the wall and leant down and kissed her like nothing else mattered. Like they were the only two people in the world. Like nothing that had just happened had just happened. Like Alexandra wasn't the future Queen of England. Her tongue pushed into Alexandra's mouth and Alexandra hungrily responded. Alexandra kissed her back like Erin was water in a desert. And she was. In a way. Alexandra had spent her life in the desert.

Erin woke up suddenly and pulled away. Suddenly reminded of the her job and their situation.

"Hold on," she said. "We need to get out of here. I need to get you out of here." She slipped her phone out of her pocket and within seconds she had ordered an Uber.

"Four minutes it says." She watched the image of the car on the map on her screen. Needed to focus on something practical. Something that wasn't Alexandra and the fact she had just kissed her. Just kissed the Princess. Was she insane? Erin felt lust coursing through her body and pooling between her legs. She couldn't look at Alexandra. She looked out of their doorway for people, for possible danger. She looked to her phone at the Uber app.

"Nearly here," she said and she took Alexandra's hand leading her out on the street to meet the car. Her eyes darted up and down the street. The street was safe. They weren't followed. She opened the door and put the Princess safely inside and then walked around the car and got in herself. She sat in the dark back seat and closed her eyes momentarily and sighed as the car began to head back to where they had left their Range Rover.

"God, that was crazy. We were lucky. I cannot believe that all happened." Erin said as the adrenaline began to crash and she felt like they were safe.

Alexandra's delicate hand reached across in the dark and held Erin's.

Her voice was vulnerable and childlike and full of gratitude. "Thank you for saving me," she said for the second time that night.

Erin closed her eyes and mentally berated herself for the stupidity of the risks she had taken that night. In amongst the frustration at herself, other moments crept into her thoughts. Flashes back to the kiss. The passion. The all encompassing desire she had felt for the Princess. The Princess asking Erin to kiss her. What on earth did this all mean?

12

Alexandra and Erin snuck back in to the palace like naughty school-girls, under cover of darkness.

"Spend some time with me?" Alexandra asked, much more herself now she was home, it was an order as much as it was a request. She headed straight into her drawing room and Erin followed like a loyal dog.

Alexandra went to her room and emerged after a couple of minutes wearing the same silk Pyjamas that Erin had seen before. Silk lounge pants and a thin ivory silk vest top with thin straps. Her eyes were striking blue again and her hair was brushed back from her face. She had never looked more desirable.

She headed over to a drinks cabinet and fridge and poured them both a gin and tonic. Tonic fizzing over ice. She handed a crystal glass to Erin.

As Erin took a deep drink she was glad of it. Glad she had stayed sober all evening but glad to taste the burning of the liquor on her tongue. She shrugged off her leather jacket and her gun and sat awkwardly on the sofa not knowing what on earth was supposed to happen next.

"I feel so safe with you." Alexandra sipped her own drink as she walked restlessly around the big room. "Thank you so much for tonight. You have no idea what it means to me; how much I enjoyed it; how free I felt."

"They might find out, you know. If they find out, I'll lose my job. I committed the absolute worst sin a bodyguard can commit, I disregarded all security protocol, I went out without backup. Nobody knew where we were."

"Why did you do it?" Alexandra asked as she stood silhouetted in the wide window.

"I find it impossible to say no to you," Erin replied honestly.

"You won't lose your job. I won't let them replace you. You are everything I want in my personal security. Everything I need. I won't let them take you from me, be assured of that." Alexandra's blue eyes fixed her in an intense gaze. "Come over here. See out of these windows, the view of the city at night."

Erin stood and walked over to the windows and immediately felt something with the closeness to the Princess. An electric chemistry sparking between them. She looked out of the window seeing the darkness of the palace grounds and then lights of the city behind them and the moon up above in a clear sky.

Alexandra stood close to her. Too close. Erin could smell the delicate feminine perfume on her.

Alexandra stood in front of her facing her and her breathing quickened.

Alexandra snaked her hand up to Erin's face and lightly pushed her hair behind her ear then ran her fingers up to Erin's eyebrow touching a faint scar just above her eyebrow.

"What happened here?" she asked.

Erin could see straight down her loose fitting silk vest from this angle and it was the most distracting view. Alexandra's breasts moving as she breathed.

"Er... oh if you are hoping for an exciting James Bond type story, it is nothing like that. I fell off a horse. Cut it open."

Alexandra ran her fingertips with a feather touch down her cheekbone and to Erin's lips. Erin's body quivered all over and her lips parted slightly at the intensity of the touch. Alexandra's fingers slipped into Erin's mouth, past her teeth, all as she held her gaze. Her fingers tasted of hand soap on Erin's tongue. She dragged them out and traced Erin's lips. Erin's neck. The muscles across the top of Erin's shoulders. Then she reached quietly onto her tiptoes and kissed Erin again. Lips against lips, against tongue, against teeth. Mouths opening to meet each other, greet each other, explore each other.

For a moment Erin was lost in it. Lost in her. Lost in the woman that Erin had been silently loving for so long. Then she pulled away sharply.

"Alexandra, you don't want this. Think about what you are doing. You've had a couple of drinks. It has been an exciting evening one way or another. This is an impulsive decision. I don't want to abuse my position or risk my job. We can stop this right here. I just want to protect you. To do my job. I don't want to push anything on you that you don't want."

Alexandra took Erin's hand and pushed it down her lounge pants. She was wearing no underwear. She interlinked their fingers and pushed Erin's fingers to her wetness. So much wetness. "I have never wanted anything more. Feel how much I want you."

Erin could feel it. There was no disputing it. Alexandra's desire, slick across both of their fingers. Then Alexandra removed her own hand and raised it again to Erin's lips. Her fingers pushing into Erin's mouth again. The taste of her, potent in Erin's mouth this time.

"Take me, Erin. I know you want me. I've seen your eyes on my body. I've seen your desire for me. Show me your world. Show me how much you want me. Take me places I have never been before."

Erin paused for just a moment and looked at her. And maybe it would be okay. Maybe there was a way for this to be. Maybe it didn't really matter what the future held, only the magic that was there in the moment. That in the moment they were just two women that wanted each other badly, had wanted each other badly for a long time.

She pushed Alexandra back against the window and kissed her. The glass panes were cold on Alexandra's back. Alexandra was responsive and passionate. A passion that her usual cool exterior hid so well day to day. Erin pulled at the silk, desperate to get to her body. Alexandra put her arms up and let Erin pull the vest over her head. Her breasts were full against her ribcage, her nipples prominent and excited. Erin still couldn't quite believe what was happening as instinctively her lips moved to Alexandra's nipples. To feel them in her mouth. To taste her skin. She ran her fingers over her body as Alexandra leant back on the wide window ledge.

Erin's hands ran under the elastic waistband of the lounge pants and Alexandra lifted her hips wanting them off. Erin wanted them off. Erin had never wanted anyone more. She pulled them down and off and here was the Princess naked in front of her reclining against the window which was steaming up with the heat from them both. Naked, not for the first time, but in entirely different circumstances. This was the Princess giving her body over. Asking to be taken. Begging to be fucked. And who was Erin to refuse that.

Erin knelt in front of her and parted Alexandra's slim thighs. Her dark blonde pubic hair formed a small neat thatch above her opening. Erin ran her mouth up the inside of Alexandra's thigh. Slightly teasing, but limited by both of their impatience. She couldn't wait any longer. Her mouth met Alexandra's burning core and her tongue lapped at her wetness knowing she would never ever get enough of the taste of her. The more her mouth worked, the wetter Alexandra got. Alexandra moaned and writhed above her. It had been years since Alexandra had felt anything like this. It had been years that Alexandra had yearned to let go, and here she was, letting it all go.

Erin pushed her face in as much as it would go. She wanted to lose herself in Alexandra in every way possible. She felt her own desire burning. She took Alexandra's clit in her mouth and sucked it gently. She felt it swell in her mouth. Alexandra's breathing quickened and her hands went to the back of Erin's head pulling her head in tighter. A red rash spread across her collarbone and breasts. She moaned loudly and she orgasmed, gushing into Erin's mouth, spilling out onto the floor.

Erin smiled to herself against Alexandra's warm stomach. Alexandra's legs were suddenly unsteady and she collapsed to the floor and into Erin's arms. Curled up, suddenly childlike and vulnerable post orgasm, she just wanted to be loved. Erin held her with her strong arms and kissed her hair and her forehead.

If Erin hadn't known already, she knew now. It probably wasn't the wisest life choice in the world but she was completely in love with this woman.

13

E rin had returned to her own room afterwards. She had wanted to stay but she needed time alone with her own thoughts. She figured they both did.

She ran her shower and pulled off her clothes, the taste of Alexandra still strong in her mouth. She stepped under the hot water and leant against the wall as she reached down and touched herself. Her own wetness. Her own lust so strong for the Princess. She hadn't let Alexandra touch her. She didn't think either of them were ready for that yet. But she was so turned on. She orgasmed hard for her own fingers with thoughts of Alexandra strong in her head. What she looked like, naked and open, her head thrown back in release. What she looked like curled up in her arms afterwards. Knowing the real Alexandra in ways that nobody else did, had become the drug she couldn't resist.

Erin groaned to herself. Nothing good could come of this love. But she knew she was completely unable to control it.

THE NEXT MORNING Erin rose and showered and headed to her morning briefing. There was a lightness to her, a smile on the edge of her lips. She breezed into the Operations Room to see Chief Inspector Evans's miserable stuffy face.

Evans was on the phone swearing at someone and didn't acknowledge her presence.

"For fuck's sake, how am I supposed to operate in these conditions?! How am I supposed to do my fucking job with fucking morons working for me? How much more stupid can someone get?"

The person at the other end of the line responded and Evans was quiet for a moment. Then he spoke again, more and more angry, his face getting redder by the minute.

"What the fuck? You have got to be fucking kidding. You cannot tie my hands like this."

"SIT," he screamed at Erin and then continued to rant into the phone.

"Idiots. Surrounded by fucking idiots. Cannot do their jobs properly. Whole Royal Family will get themselves fucking kidnapped and assassinated if we carry on like this."

He slammed the phone down and grunted loudly, his displeasure evident. Then he spun around to face Erin. His voice suddenly toned down and dripping with sarcasm.

"Sergeant Kennedy. So good of you to join us. This morning, I have a video I need you to watch." He slid his laptop across the table.

"Press Play."

Erin clicked on play and saw a CCTV image start to play out in front of her. Her heart dropped like a stone and she felt sick as she saw what was on the video.

"Kennedy," he said. A statement or a question she was unsure.

"KENNEDY," he shouted at her.

"Yes, Sir," she responded robotically.

He pressed pause on the recording and used his fat finger to point at one of the people on the screen.

"Why don't you tell me who this fucking idiot here is?"

Erin closed her eyes in despair and mumbled, "It's me."

"WHAT?" he boomed. "I didn't fucking hear you."

"It's me, Sir." she said louder.

"Why don't you tell me who this is here? This lady cleverly disguised in a dark wig."

"It's Princess Alexandra, Sir."

"Now, why don't you tell me what the fuck you and the fucking Princess were doing galavanting around Soho last night with no backup? All of us thinking you two are safely tucked up in bed, then I get this fucking phone call and this fucking CCTV recording of my officer assaulting a member of the public, putting the Princess at huge risk, disobeying literally every rule in fucking Security 101. How the fuck do I explain to the Metropolitan Police and the Security Services why the fuck the future fucking queen is out and about in Soho, of all places, unprotected, with no back up and why my officer is such a fucking MORON?!!!!!"

He continued.

"What the fuck did you think would happen? What the fuck did you think you were going to do if anyone recognised her? If some shit went down, some real shit I mean, not this fucking pathetic beating up of some unarmed pissed guy. Who do you think you are? Lara fucking Croft?"

"I'm sorry," Erin said, her head low. She knew that she had literally been caught in the act here. That there was no going back. Why on earth hadn't she thought there might be CCTV on the street? Yet there it was, as clear as day, a replay of the exact moments of last night. Only, in the replay there was no sound. There was no justification for her actions. His comments weren't recorded. It just looked like him drunkenly lumbering in to the Princess, pulling her wig off accidentally, and Erin responding with the brutality at which she would defend a knife attack and attacking this guy. The only thing Erin was grateful for is there was no video of what happened afterwards. No video of the kiss.

"I.... I...... er..... The Princess asked me to keep her secrets. She wanted to go out without backup. What was I supposed to say?"

"No would have been good. Fucking NO. Would that have been so hard? The correct answer is fucking No. I'm very sorry Ma'am, but I cannot guarantee your safety without backup, this goes against all security protocol and I just cannot jeopardise your safety like that. Yadda Yadda Yadda..... NO." He looked expectantly to Erin, his tiny piggy eyes evil in his big face.

"I'm sorry." Erin knew this was an immediately fireable offence. Erin knew this was it, her whole career over because of one dumb mistake. Because she was too in love with Alexandra to say no to her. If she lost this job, she would never see Alexandra again. That much was clear.

"You should be gone Kennedy. Gone, faster than I can fill in the fucking paperwork. Never in my career have I seen such fucking moronic actions. Never have I ever seen such fucking stupidity. If it was up to me, your sorry ass would never ever work for any kind of Police or security job ever again. Maybe standing at the door of a supermarket watching for shoplifters. Maybe that is something you could be fucking capable of. Something suited to a fucking idiot like you. Knew there was a reason girls shouldn't do this job. You haven't got a fucking brain in your pretty little head."

She raised her head. Maybe there was still hope. He said, if it was up to him. Maybe it isn't up to him.

"However." He took a deep breath. Clearly, what he was about to say was going to be difficult for him.

"The powers that be have decided that what Princess Fucking Alexandra wants, she fucking gets. And right now, she wants you, and unfortunately none of the powers that be are ballsy enough to tell her she can't have you anymore. So. One way or another, you are still in a job. But, grow a fucking brain Kennedy. This isn't a fucking joke. Do you want to be responsible for something happening to the heir to the throne? How do you think the fucking king will feel about that? You think he is going to let you get away with pulling these kind of stunts if he finds out about it? You are on thin ice Kennedy. Thin fucking ice. Tread carefully. Tread very fucking carefully. Luckily for you, I've made the whole last night situation go away. The CCTV original is fucking gone. But, one more slip up and none of us will protect you. Capisce?"

"I understand," said Erin, humbly. And she did. For once, she almost agreed with Evans. She had fucked up, well and truly. She was lucky that in doing so, in taking all those risks, nothing bad had happened to Alexandra. Her love for Alexandra, her inability to say no to Alexandra, had lead to her taking stupid risks. Thinking that it was ok to take stupid risks.

"Now, get out of my fucking sight. And don't forget today's fucking schedule." He jabbed at a folder on the table that she picked up and got out of the door as fast as she could.

BY THE TIME Erin had made it through her gym session and some unarmed combat training and back to the Princess's rooms, things were a flurry of activity. Alicia doing Alexandra's hair. Jess busying around. Natalie laying out clothes.

"Morning Erin," they each called to her.

"Erin," called Alexandra. Erin liked her own name so much more when it came from Alexandra's lips. She caught Alexandra's clear blue eyes in the reflection from the mirror. "Please do help yourself to some breakfast, I've had quite a lot sent up, I didn't know what you would want."

Business as usual.

Erin looked to the big table, loaded with breakfast options. There were cooked breakfast options under stainless steel domes. An assortment of fruits, breads and pastries. She helped herself to a plate of Eggs Benedict and a banana. She wasn't sure she was strictly hungry after everything that had happened last night and this morning, but in this job, eating where you could was always important. You never knew when you would get the opportunity again. Similarly going to the toilet. Take the opportunity where it presents itself. You cannot exactly abandon the Princess when you are out and about while you go and find a toilet or some food.

Alexandra was carrying on as though nothing had ever happened. Erin slipped straight back into professional mode too. It was her only option. She tortured herself wondering what the Princess was thinking. What she was feeling after last night. Wondering when she would ever get the opportunity to be alone with her again to talk openly, or maybe something more.

Erin hoped that Alexandra didn't regret what had happened. If she regretted it, she wouldn't hesitate to get rid of Erin. To replace her. Had Erin crossed a line? Had Erin taken advantage while Alexandra had been drinking? God, she hoped not.

ALEXANDRA HAD a public appearance and a meeting later that day and Erin accompanied her loyally. Doing her job to the letter.

Not one foot out of place. Alexandra barely looked at her. Erin dully accepted her place in the world as Alexandra's shadow. Not her girlfriend or potential girlfriend. Not even as someone casually being used for sex. She worked for Alexandra, it was her job to protect her. She was kidding herself if she thought there was anything else there.

14

A couple of days passed and Alexandra was still distant and cold. Professional and painfully polite to Erin. Erin swallowed her pain and did her job. She wished she had someone she could talk to about this but she wasn't really close to anyone. The nature of her work had distanced her from her friends. Even so, who could she say this to?

Oh by the way I fucked Princess Alexandra. Yes, that one. The heir to the British throne. Yes, my boss. Yes. And I think I am in love with her. And now she is ignoring me and pretending it didn't happen. What do I do?

Not something she could say.

No way. Under no circumstances could she confide in anyone over this. She had signed all manner of Non Disclosure Agreements and the Official Secrets Act. This was her secret to bear. This was as big of a secret that there is.

She wished she could visit Alexandra late at night and talk to her. Separated only by a couple of doors, it seemed so possible. But, it just wasn't protocol. She couldn't approach the Princess unless requested to.

She wanted to text her. But every time she thought of it and composed it, she decided she was insane and deleted it. You cannot just text her because you feel like it. You only have the privilege of her phone number for important work reasons. Abuse of that privilege, in fact, anything to piss off Alexandra and Erin would be replaced, faster than she could say replaced.

ALEXANDRA HAD a meeting scheduled on Thursday with her father, the King. She walked alone through the palace to meet him. They weren't a close family at all. He was a very solitary man. He lived in his own chambers, separate even from Alexandra's mother, his wife. They were still officially together. They attended public functions together, but they lived very separately. Alexandra's mother chose to spend a lot of her time in her own living quarters and with her big group of friends. Alexandra wasn't close to her mother either. She found her mother harboured a lot of jealousy since Alexandra had become an adult. Jealousy at Alexandra's future and the power that she held. It isn't the natural way of things. The respect your elder line doesn't work when your child is heir to the throne. Alexandra knew that she used her status to her advantage when it suited her. She liked the power she held.

Alexandra knocked on the door to her father's private rooms. She was met by a servant, who bowed to her and lead her to her father's study. The ceremony of tradition and rules was always obeyed.

King George sat behind his large desk and he looked older. Every time she saw him lately, he looked older. More worn down by life and by his responsibilities. Alexandra bowed her head to him.

"Father," she said.

"Alexandra, welcome."

Her father's assistant, Henry sat beside him, as he had for many many years. He was as familiar to Alexandra as her father was. They greeted each other.

"Alexandra," the King began. "Please do update me on your marriage situation. I understand you have met with one of the suggested candidates and spoken with others. It is my understanding that a front runner has emerged in Prince Nicolas."

"I have read the files on all the men you suggested. The only one I thought might be suitable is Prince Nicolas. So, I have met with him a couple of times and got to know him." Alexandra spoke dutifully and reflectively.

"He seems very suitable Alexandra. And a marriage with him will greatly improve our relations with Sweden. It would be a very beneficial arrangement. How do you find him, personally."

"I find him kind and respectful, Father."

"Have you approached the subject of marriage with him?"

"I haven't. Not yet. I have focussed on getting to know him. But he is not a stupid man. He will understand what the purpose of our getting to know each other is about."

"Indeed Alexandra, I am sure he will. He would jump at the opportunity, I'm sure. As would any of these men. A marriage to you and the future you would give them would benefit them more than they could ever imagine. I will meet him. Henry, you will arrange a dinner. Alexandra you will attend too, alongside your mother. We must all meet him. Subject to my approval, you will discuss engagement with him, or Henry can do it on your behalf. Either way, the legal implications, the details, what is and what isn't going to be put in the marriage contract will be discussed between Henry and Nicolas and his advisors."

"I understand, Father."

"I hear you have also ended things with Lord Hugo. Do you want the palace to put out an official statement to this effect?"

"Please do, Father."

"Wonderful. I will see you soon,

Alexandra. As soon as we are able to organise this dinner with Nicolas."

He looked back to his paperwork and Alexandra knew that the meeting was over and she was dismissed.

Henry jumped up and showed her to the door.

Alexandra thought again about the tall blonde Nicolas. A kind man. A respectful man, she hoped. What would their marriage be like?

15

They hadn't been out that day. Alexandra had met with her father, but Erin had spent the day on Netflix. Filling the dull emptiness in her soul.

Everything was quiet, it was late evening, all the staff had been sent home. Erin's phone beeped. A text from Alexandra:

> *Erin, please come and meet me in my apartment as soon as you are able*

Erin read it three times.
No way.

What on earth did Alexandra want at this time of night?

She text back:

Sure. Should I bring anything? Do you want to go out? Should I let the team know? What should I wear?

Her phone beeped again:

Come as you are, I don't want to go anywhere, I just want some company. No need to inform anyone else.

What did she want? Erin had no idea. Alexandra had basically ignored her for five days since that night.

Erin was just wearing a tight vest top and underwear and she was in bed. She couldn't go over in this. What on earth should she wear? She thought for a minute and then pulled on her joggers. Just something casual. She didn't want to look like she had been sitting in her room fully dressed. Should she put a bra on? She looked at herself in the mirror, just another sporty lesbian. Such a cliche. She decided not to wear a bra. It would be trying too hard. It wasn't like her breasts were big enough for it to be an issue.

She padded out of her room in her bare feet and headed to Alexandra's drawing room where Alexandra waited in more silk Pyjamas. This time in a rich dark red. Like red wine. Or blood. Erin, yet again, was struck by her beauty. Erin had never seen anyone more beautiful than her and every time it surprised her. She liked this time the best. This natural pyjama time where Alexandra wasn't overdone with make up and expensive clothes.

"Erin, thank you for coming," she said, her voice soft and magical. "I know I have been distant the past few days and for that, I can only apologise. There is something I want to do, to make it up to you, but this isn't an order. You aren't at work now. This is me, asking you, as a friend. Please, I will completely understand if you say no. Please say no if you don't want to. I promise that I won't be offended. It will not affect your job in any way. I would very much like for you to stay in my service."

Erin looked surprised and confused by Alexandra's words.

"I mean. I don't know. I understand why you were distant. You don't have to apologise to me. What is it you want to do?" Erin felt awkward and her body showed it.

Alexandra walked over to her and took her hand. Her touch was electric to Erin, she felt it everywhere. Alexandra lead her through one door and another, to her bedroom door. She opened the door to a room from a film. To a fairy land. The four poster bed was magical anyway, but the room was scattered with rose petals, red interrupting the white. There were candles lit everywhere. More candles than Erin had ever seen. They were scented or the petals were, or maybe both, and the sweet scent of roses filled the room.

Alexandra looked her directly in the eyes and said, "I want to give you a massage. If you consent. Only if you consent. Please don't feel like this is something you have to do. Please don't see this as an order. I never ever want you to feel like I am taking advantage of my power and position."

"Wow….. um…… I mean, I really wasn't expecting this. I don't know what to say. Nobody has ever offered me anything like this before. The room, it is so beautiful. Did you do it all yourself?"

"Yes. I mean I had help sourcing the rose petals and the candles in these quantities. But yes, I set it up myself. I wanted to do something special for you. I have some special massage oil. I have warmed it through for you, it smells amazing." Alexandra was intent, like a child. She had done this thing and she wanted Erin to appreciate it.

And Erin did. She was blown away by the effort. She felt uncomfortable with the idea of being so vulnerable to someone, but she wanted to try.

"Ok. Sure…. I mean, I should be honest in that I feel a bit awkward about it. But I want to. Sure."

Alexandra smiled at her and moved closer to her. She began to remove Erin's clothes.

"Put your arms up." Alexandra spoke to her as though she was a child as she pulled Erin's vest up over her head. Erin felt suddenly exposed, her breasts open to Alexandra for the first time, but she trusted the Princess. Her nipples stood erect with excitement and gooseflesh pimpled her skin.

Alexandra leant down and pulled her joggers down over her hips. Slowly, purposefully, they dropped to her ankles and Alexandra pulled them over each foot individually, Erin laughing as she lost balance and had to use Alexandra's shoulders as support.

Erin stood in only her underwear and thought Alexandra would stop there. But she didn't. She moved to the elastic of Erin's briefs, her thumbs in the elastic on each hip. Then she looked up to Erin as if for permission. Erin could have stopped her if she wanted to. But she realised that she didn't want to. Alexandra pulled her underwear down and off over her feet exposing her small neat strip of dark pubic hair. Erin had never felt so vulnerable or turned on.

"Lie face down on the bed." A request. Or an order. Either way, it was one that Erin obeyed willingly, crawling inside the white drapes and positioning herself face down on the bed amongst the rose petals.

"Are roses your favourite? Is that where your security code name comes from?" she asked, her voice muffled by the duvet.

"Yes. I have always loved roses. I love the sweet scent of them. As a child I would play in the palace rose gardens and pick the petals. I would mash them with water and make perfume from the roses. I cut my hands often on the thorns. But even the sight of my own blood never spoilt my enjoyment of the rose gardens. I still go there sometimes. They are my favourite places."

Alexandra clicked on some relaxing music. Erin had never been in an atmosphere more serene. The candlelight flickered, soft lighting over her naked body. She felt calmer about it than she would have imagined.

Alexandra enjoyed watching her body bathed in the flickering light. The tight, muscular lines of Erin's body that Alexandra had been secretly watching for months now, were suddenly all exposed for her.

She took in the strength of Erin's back,

the roundness of her glutes, her defined hamstrings. The work she did in the gym daily had not gone to waste.

Alexandra climbed on the bed next to Erin, made herself comfortable and poured warm oil onto Erin's back. Erin flinched momentarily before her body adjusted to it and it felt warm and nice.

Then there were Alexandra's hands, smooth and delicate. Working themselves into the oil and up and down the muscles of Erin's back, along her arms, to every muscle, to her hands. Paying special attention to her hands, massaging the slippery oil into each and every finger and across her palm. It felt incredible. Erin could hear Alexandra's breathing alongside the music as she worked hard on Erin's back. She felt Alexandra's warm hands as they crept around her ribcage, brushing the sides of her breasts. She felt her warm hands as they rubbed oil smoothly around her hips, her pelvis, moving down to her ass.

She expected Alexandra to bypass her ass cheeks, as a professional masseuse normally does, so she almost jumped in surprise when she felt more warm oil being poured over her ass. It ran down the crack, teasing her everywhere. She felt Alexandra's hands working into each cheek and down to the back of her thighs. The inside of her thighs. Slippery hands sliding everywhere. Brushing against her clit, almost as if it was an accident.

But, it was no accident. Erin was sure.

Alexandra's hands continued on their quest. Firm strokes down over the length of her legs. From ass, to leg, to foot and back again. Alexandra moving quietly above her with the grace of a dancer.

Alexandra rubbed her feet. Between her toes. Erin felt it everywhere. Alexandra's warm oily hands were doing things to her body that she had never imagined. Her body was responding to the Princess's hands.

Erin was wet. So so wet.

Alexandra's hands slid back up to Erin's ass. Her hands firm. Her hands soft. Her hands teasing and taunting. They explored further. She touched every part of Erin. Brushing across her clit, her opening, teasing her anus. Alexandra's fingers were the bringer of magic.

Erin began to lose herself in it, to finally relax out of her head and lose herself in the feeling of the moment. The heat began to build and her head felt dizzy as Alexandra's slippery fingers worked more insistently, over her, teasing and inside.

Then her mind exploded into a kaleidoscope of colour and her body shook as she came.

Alexandra got on top of her and lay on her back. The silk of her pyjamas the only thing between them.

Alexandra's lips to her shoulder kissing her gently, nuzzling her neck. Her lips to Erin's ear.

"I've wanted to do that to you for so long," she whispered.

Erin's mind was blown post orgasm.

"I just need a minute," she stuttered.

"Take all the time in the world. Please, I just want you to relax. You work so hard. This is about you."

Erin lay still, unable to move, and Alexandra got up and went to the bathroom. She ran a bath and scattered rose petals in the warm water. She was excited to finally get use of her big bath with someone she wanted to share it with. It was a big traditional free standing tub with two high ends for sitting against.

She waited for Erin to regain consciousness and then lead her gently to the bath and helped her in. She stripped her own pyjamas off and Erin looked up and marvelled at her body as she climbed in beside her. Erin at one end and Alexandra at the other, their legs seductively intertwined under bubbles and rose petals.

"I never would have thought this. I never would have imagined it was possible. I mean, I dreamt it, sure. But I never thought it could be real. Being naked in a bath with you." Erin stuttered.

"Oh, it's real Erin. I have been dreaming it for a while too. But, I had to be sure. I had to know for sure I could trust you. And I can."

"Oh you can. With anything. I've risked everything for you. Well, I am risking everything now I guess too, by being with you. Don't sleep with your principal is one of the first rules of Close Protection. Learn them, know them by heart, but never get too close. I'd lose my job if anyone found out." She relaxed her head back under the bubbles, soaking her hair and face and then coming up for air, her wet dark hair clinging to her head and shoulders.

"I'd lose everything if anyone found out," Alexandra said matter of factly.

"Can't you do whatever you like?" Erin knew she was being naive as she said it. "You know, being the future queen and all that."

"Oh, I wish it was that easy." The Princess sighed. "You can see how limited my life is. You watch me every day. You see the limits I have on my freedom."

"Why not change things? You could, you know. You could do anything."

"The people need to see a certain image from the Royal Family. From their future leader. There's just things that are expected. Things that I was born into. Things that cannot change. I wish, I really wish things were different. So many times I have imagined being born into a normal family, living a normal life. You and I are pretty much the same age, and look at all the things that you have achieved and are capable of that I never could. "

Erin laughed. "Like what?! You are one of the most famous women in the world!"

"Oh Erin, you don't see yourself like I do. You have ridden at a high level, worked at some of the biggest horse competitions that there are. You can fight, you can shoot, you have pursued a tough career and excelled in it. Protecting someone like me is as good as it gets in your industry surely? I feel so safe with you by my side. You are so impressive."

Erin smiled. She had never seen things in that way. Chief Inspector Evans didn't think she was impressive. He thought she was a moron. Erin was hardest on herself though. Erin held herself to such high standards every day that it was no wonder that she never impressed herself. Maybe it was constantly fighting to be seen in a male dominated world? Maybe it was always having to be that little bit better at something to be recognised as a woman.

"I think being Princess Alexandra is pretty impressive." Erin responded, her eyes dark with lazy desire.

"Princess Alexandra is a rank I was

born to. That is just luck. It isn't impressive."

"Oh, Alexandra. Being Princess Alexandra is SO much more than that. I watch you every day playing that role. It is a lifetime of acting, of being so perfect and kind and genuine. It is a lifetime of remembering the little people's names, of saying thank you, of being humble, of caring when you don't really care. It is a world of giving parts of yourself away a hundred times a day and wondering if there will be anything real left in the end." Erin took a breath. "You are incredible. Every day. That is why you are the most loved Princess. You are what changes perceptions of the Royal Family."

"Thank you. You see a lot. Before you, I'm not sure when anyone else last saw the real me. I'm not really sure what is left of the real me. Anyway. Enough of this emotional stuff. You are making me blush!" Her cheeks pinked up endearingly.

Alexandra splashed Erin to lighten the moment. Erin splashed back. They both laughed.

"I can't believe you just splashed me,

you bitch!" Erin laughed, leaning forwards and grabbing Alexandra playfully.

Alexandra just laughed. "Let go, let go," she laughed with bubbles in her face. "Did you just call your future queen a bitch?"

"Um....... No. You must have misheard." Erin was on top of Alexandra at her end now, glad of the space in the big bath as she pinned the Princess against the back of the bath and kissed her intensely.

"I've been wanting to do that again. So much."

Alexandra felt herself weaken and go to mush. Nothing was more seductive to her than Erin's strength above her.

"I want to feel you inside me," Alexandra whispered. "I want it so much. I've never done it before."

"What do you mean?"

"Penetration, I've never received it before. I've only been with one woman, a long time ago, and she never did that to me. I fantasise about it all the time."

"I'll look after you. There's nothing I want to give you more," Erin held her.

Erin didn't need asking twice. She was on her knees, straddling Alexandra's hips as she kissed her and pushed her right hand under the water between Alexandra's legs.

Alexandra's labia opened to welcome her hand and she felt her slickness immediately across her fingers even under the water. Erin touched and teased while her tongue explored Alexandra's mouth with an intensity that Alexandra had never felt.

Her finger pushed inside Alexandra whose pupils dilated as she felt it. She slipped back almost under the water in delight and Erin rescued her with her strong left arm.

"You had better keep your head above water if you want more. I can't have Princess Alexandra accidentally drowning in my care!"

Alexandra giggled and nodded. "I want more. Please more. Please, I need you, so much."

Erin pushed another finger inside, feeling her body adjust to accommodate the fingers. Alexandra moaned in appreciation and she pushed towards the fingers. Out and in again. Out and in again.

Alexandra went crazy beneath her, moaning, begging.

"Please, please, that feels so good. That feels like nothing else on earth."

Erin curled her fingers upwards to reach Alexandra's G spot and continued with the in and out, increasing tempo.

Alexandra writhed and moaned beneath her. Louder. Vocal in her appreciation as Erin moved her hand faster, harder, more insistently.

Alexandra moved her own fingers to her clitoris while Erin fucked her. Seconds after touching herself, she dissolved into orgasm underneath Erin. Her eyes closed, her body tensed and then went limp. The orgasm rash appeared again across the top of her breasts and collarbone. Erin had never seen anything more beautiful.

THEY LAY in Alexandra's luxurious bed for a time afterwards talking. About nothing. About everything. Erin couldn't stay over and fall asleep there, she knew that really. She wished the hours would slow. That she could stay there forever with Alexandra in her arms, but she knew she couldn't. If she was caught there, they would both be in so much trouble.

As she saw the first light of dawn threatening at the edges of the curtains she knew she had to leave. She kissed Alexandra again and snuck out quietly, returning to her own bed where she lay alone and thoughtful.

What on earth was happening between her and the Princess? Where on earth could this go?

16

Weeks later it was scheduled for the Royal Family to visit Sweden to meet with Prince Nicolas and his family. Alexandra knew that preliminary discussions about their potential marriage would have already happened between advisors for both families.

That was a strange thought really.

That someone else was discussing her marriage with her future husband before she had discussed it with him. She felt more comfortable with someone else discussing it with him.

Also, meanwhile, she had been busy fucking her bodyguard late every evening under the cover of darkness. It felt crazy really. Every evening Alexandra would text Erin and get her to come round. She wanted her. She needed her. She wanted to be her real self and the only way she felt able to do that was alone with Erin. She wanted to learn everything about Erin, and have Erin learn everything about her. What she was doing, she didn't know, but they were both lost in it. Sleep had become a stranger. They were too lost in each other.

Security was arranged in advance and they flew on the Royal plane.

Alexandra had demanded that Erin was put in a room adjoining her own and on arrival at the Swedish palace she was pleased with her room arrangements. As she requested. Away from her family and next to Erin.

Alexandra got ready with Alicia in her room for dinner with Nicolas and his family. She slid into a lovely long Prussian blue evening gown. It brought out her eyes. She knew it suited her. Alicia did her make up and hair and then she dismissed her.

She had ten minutes before she was due at dinner so she texted Erin.

Come to me

Erin didn't question or even respond to Alexandra's requests for her presence any more. She was literally waiting for any moment they could be alone together. There were never enough moments.

Erin knocked.

"Come in."

"You look incredible, Alex," Erin was taken aback every time she looked at Alexandra. She wished with everything she had that it could be her accompanying Alexandra to dinner.

She moved straight to kiss Alexandra but Alexandra pushed her off and laughed.

"Look at my makeup. Look at this lipstick... you can't kiss me!"

Erin looked confused momentarily and frustratedly pretended to bite and kiss at Alexandra's neck and collarbone. Pulling her into her arms, biting feather lightly at her so her mouth wouldn't leave any marks.

Her perfume was overpowering and made Erin heady with desire.

"I've got no underwear on," whispered Alexandra breathily.

Erin's eyes widened with want.

"You've got five minutes. Literally 5 minutes," Alexandra giggled as Erin's lips and tongue tickled her neck.

Erin didn't need asking twice. She lifted Alexandra's long blue dress and her right hand began to explore.

She was so wet. So wanting.

Erin pushed immediately inside her and Alexandra's body responded. This was something Alexandra had gone from never having done, to having totally discovered her G spot and wanting it all the time. She craved to be fucked by Erin's strong fingers all the time. Her back arched over Erin's left arm as Erin began to fuck her.

Erin wanted to take her in every way possible and feast on her body for hours.

But for now, for this five minutes, Alexandra needed hard and fast. She wanted to come fast for the incomparable feeling of Erin's fingers inside her. They were beginning to learn each other. Beginning to learn the other's body. To be grabbed and taken as Erin was doing now was something that drove Alexandra wild. She was discovering all kinds of sexual freedom.

She moaned into Erin's shoulder as she came hard and soaked Erin's hand.

"Fuck. Your dress!" Erin laughed and pulled the dress up further with her left hand to avoid staining it.

"Towel, towel, we need a towel." She looked around frantically as Alexandra purred contentedly, her eyes glazed. Literally Erin's left hand holding her dress tight felt like the only thing holding her up. Erin grabbed a cushion as she leant Alexandra against the sofa and used the cushion to soak up the excess wetness and dry the inside of her thighs.

Alexandra just laughed.

"Sorry about the cushion." Erin chucked it back on the sofa. "It was the only thing to hand. Lucky cushion!"

"Stop laughing, you'll be late for dinner!"

"Sorry Sergeant Kennedy," Alexandra said seductively as she pulled her dress back down and rearranged herself in the mirror.

"You look so so very beautiful."

"Come and see me later. Please. I'll need you again. I have to go now." Alexandra blew a kiss as she made her way out of the door.

Erin sat on the arm of the sofa, next to the wet cushion, dazed with what had happened.

She had awoken some animal passion deep inside Alexandra and that in turn had awoken something similar within herself. It was driving them both crazy with desire.

Every night for the past few weeks they had done a similar dance. Alexandra texting late on and requesting her company. Then losing themselves in each other's bodies for hours.

How she was going to cope with Alexandra spending the evening with her future husband, she did not know.

She brought her right hand to her lips and smelt the potency of Alexandra's sex.

She licked her fingers clean, tasting every bit of Alexandra's come.

She tipped her head back and sighed loudly.

Princess Alexandra. What are you doing to me?

17

"Nicolas, so lovely to see you again." Alexandra was effusive in her greeting and dazzling in her long blue dress.

"And you, you look so very beautiful Princess. It is an honour to have you and your family to stay with us. You are absolutely glowing." Nicolas looked at her intently, yet kindly with his pale eyes. Nicolas was impeccably presented in suit of the darkest navy blue, which coincidentally matched her dress very well.

She smiled to herself. Glowing because of the incredible orgasm her bodyguard had just given her.

"Mother. Father." Erin greeted her parents warmly as they approached.

"Alexandra. Always a pleasure," said King George. "And Prince Nicolas. A pleasure to make your acquaintance. I look forward to knowing you further."

Alexandra tuned herself out to the small talk. She could do it in her sleep. Polite. Friendly. Dazzling when she smiled. Interested in everyone. She gave them all what they wanted from her as her thoughts strayed to thoughts of Erin and she felt her own wetness trickle down her inner thighs.

The dinner passed uneventfully. She learnt more about Nicolas and his family as dinner finished and everyone dispersed, Nicolas and Alexandra were left at the table alone talking for hours. She liked him. They got on well together.

"Alexandra, will you come back with me to my rooms? I would very much like to spend some time alone with you."

"Of course," she responded, almost warily, hoping more than anything that he didn't try and touch her.

∾

"YOUR APARTMENT IS LOVELY, NICOLAS." Alexandra took in the bold masculine decor and was happy to praise him. She took her gin and sat on the large dark grey sofa that dominated the room.

"So," said Nicolas as he sat down next to her. He only had a marginal accent. His English was as proper as Alexandra's own. "I would like to discuss the matter in hand with you, if that is okay?"

Alexandra nodded.

"The possibility of our marriage is something that I would be very happy about Alexandra. I am not deluded enough to think that my status is in any way in the same league as your own, however I do think that I would make the perfect compliment to you. Between us we would make such a royal power couple. I'll add enough status, but never too much that it would in any way eclipse your own light. I want to stand beside you as you become Queen, Alexandra. I am happy to always be in the background. To always live in your shadow."

"How do you feel about children Nicolas? I understand my father's advisor has requested that you undergo some tests?"

"Yes. And I have. My sperm is of good quality. There should be no reason it could not be used to create a pregnancy. And I want children. Deeply. My main focus for marriage is to continue both of our family lines. As I am sure it is for you too."

"Yes. Very much so. My family and my country. They both need this. They both need this from me." Alexandra sighed.

"Alexandra, there is something I want to address. It is difficult for me to speak about, but I feel we must be open with each other."

Alexandra raised her eyes to him, curious to hear what he was about to say.

"I think you are only interested in this marriage purely as an arrangement. I can sense that you aren't interested in a love with me. I can sense that you aren't interested in me in that way."

"Wait.. .I am. I ... I...."

"Let me speak," Nicolas continued. "Let me speak openly, and I would appreciate if you would do me the honour and respect of speaking honestly in return. The thing is, this is precisely why I am so keen to marry you. I consider myself largely asexual. I have no real interest in sex or romance. Our marriage would be very much for the public eye. I would like to have a strong friendship with you and I would love more than anything to become a father, although this may have to be achieved artificially. I would always be very respectful of you and I don't have any other sinister secrets, other than this. I don't feel able to ever come out openly about this. I am afraid of public perception. I would dearly like to marry and bear children in the hope that this never be shown to the world. I realise that this is a lot to take on board and I very much encourage you to take your time and have a think about this from your point of view and consider if this is a life that you would choose. I don't know your motivations for wanting this arrangement, but I assume you have your own reasons for wanting a marriage with someone you aren't in love with. I don't need to know them now. However, all I ask is your honesty and respect."

Alexandra was taken aback by his openness and she sat for a moment reflectively.

"Thank you for your openness Nicolas. I can assure you, your words will go no further. You are right in that I am not in love with you, nor do I have interest in you in that way. And I find myself relieved at the realisation that our potential children would be conceived artificially. I have my reasons, which I am not ready to discuss just yet and I am not sure that I ever will be. However, I am so grateful for the kindness and respect you have shown me throughout and they are qualities in you that stand out for me in my search for a husband. Let me think about your words. Let me think about our possible future together."

Nicolas smiled and touched her hand. "Thank you very much Alexandra. I appreciate your confidentiality and I genuinely see a great future between us."

18

Alexandra returned to her room and sat quietly, knowing Erin would have heard her return but not sure that she wanted to see her yet. Alexandra's burden, although it should have felt lighter following Nicolas's confession, it somehow also felt heavier and more real. Her marriage. Her children. Could she find a way to carry on fucking her bodyguard in secret? Was that really what she wanted with Erin, sordid quickies where she could get them?

She sighed and collapsed backwards onto her bed.

She knew she should see Erin and talk

to her. It was 3am. Dinner had run late, and then she had spent time talking to Nicolas, maybe Erin would be asleep.

Alexandra kicked off her shoes and wandered barefoot to Erin's room pushing the door open and seeing Erin sitting up in bed in the dark. She looked like she had been crying even though Erin wasn't someone she imagined ever crying.

"Erin..." she started quietly.

"Did you have sex with him, Alex? Please. I need to know. I thought I would be okay with this. I thought I would find a way to cope. But as the hours wore on and you didn't return, I started going out of my head. Sorry, I shouldn't ask. It isn't my business. Oh god, I shouldn't have said any of this." Erin's emotions spilled out of her mouth like water.

"Shhh. Shhhh. Sweetheart, no. I didn't do it. I promise."

Erin looked up, her eyes black in the dark. "You didn't? What happened?"

"We just talked." Alexandra repeated word for word to Erin, exactly what Nicolas had confessed to her.

Erin laughed. Spluttered. "Seriously?!"

"I think he was very serious, yes. Which makes him the perfect husband for me. My marriage to him will enable us to carry on spending time alone with each other where we can."

Erin looked thoughtful.

"The thing is. The thing I'm just struggling with, Alex, is I don't know if I can do this. Will you have made me sleep in the bedroom next to you both? Will I ever get time alone with you? A few snatched moments here and there?"

"Erin, no, no." Alexandra climbed on the bed, hitched her dress up and straddled Erin. "It won't be like that, I promise. It won't be like that. We will find a way." She kissed Erin deeply and Erin pushed her away.

"I can't Alex, I don't think I can."

"This is good news. Obviously I will have to share a bed with him but we won't have sex. This will be so much better, Erin, I promise."

Alexandra kissed her again and Erin started crying and looked away and beat at Alexandra weakly with her fists.

It didn't hurt, Alexandra knew she

wasn't really trying at all, she was breaking inside. Her big strong bodyguard was suddenly weak as a kitten beneath her and it was all her fault.

Alexandra gripped both of her wrists and pushed them back against the pillow and kissed Erin. Her hair, her face, her tears salty on her tongue. She licked at Erin's cheeks, kissing away the tears. She kissed lightly along Erin's jawbone. Erin still crying and pathetically resisting. They both knew that Erin was strong enough to throw her off in one movement if she really wanted to. Alexandra kissed down her neck and up to her earlobe. Taking her earlobe in her mouth and sucking it. Kissing around her ear, pushing her tongue into her ear.

"I love you," she whispered. "I love you Erin."

Erin's eyes widened in shock and she stopped crying momentarily. Then she cried again.

"I don't know if I can do it. I don't think I can. I hate watching you with him. I hate imagining you with him."

Alexandra kissed down over her collarbone, pushing the duvet down. Erin was naked beneath the duvet, her breasts suddenly exposed and Alexandra went straight to her nipple with her lips, kissing, suckling. Erin's body started responding involuntarily, her nipples erect, her skin flushed and excited.

Alexandra pushed further, kissing down over her taut abdominal muscles, a stomach that was built to envy.

"I love you, Erin. I love you." She kept saying it. She kept kissing. She ran her tongue down over Erin's hipbones, down to her groin.

"I love you, Erin. We will find a way through this." She pushed Erin's legs roughly apart and buried her face between them. Her tongue insistent. Her mouth firm and wanting.

Erin looked down between tears to find Alexandra's beautiful golden head bobbing between her legs. Her eyes were closed. She was hard at work for Erin's pleasure. Erin's clit responding against her will, swelling up with excitement in Alexandra's mouth. Erin felt Alexandra's fingers pushing their way into her and she suddenly needed them more than anything in the world. She arched her back and pushed onto the fingers. She grabbed the back of Alexandra's head and pushed into her face. She ground into Alexandra's mouth and fingers and her world exploded into a million pieces.

They stayed there for a time as Erin came round from her orgasm and Alexandra lay between her legs, her face lying gently on top of Erin's pelvis, breathing in the sweet scent of Erin's pleasure. Tears dried on Erin's cheeks.

Alex, you are destroying me.

19

The next morning when Erin rose, exhausted from emotion, she heard Alicia babbling away to Alexandra as she did her makeup.

"Morning Erin. How are you doing?" Alicia was annoyingly upbeat.

"Ah, pretty tired. I didn't sleep so well to be honest."

"It is exciting about the Princess and Prince Nicolas isn't it? I cannot wait. I love weddings! I have SO many ideas for hair and makeup I cannot tell you. I cannot wait to see the dress you choose."

Alexandra smiled wryly into the mirror.

Erin took a deep breath. "I'm sure the

Princess will look nothing less than in-credible."

Alicia seemed immune to the pain in Erin's voice. "So, ma'am, I was thinking we could curl it and pin it up some-thing like this." She pulled Alexandra's hair up in pieces off her face, her beau-tiful face. Erin couldn't bear to look. "We can get some fake hair to clip in if you want some length and it will look fuller in an updo. Nobody will ever know. Fake hair is SO good these days. I'll get some to match your colour exactly."

Alexandra was very silent compared to her usual self. Alicia, however was deter-mined to fill the silence.

"Ma'am, what time will we be leaving today? What are your plans?" Erin asked. Their schedule and protection over here was being handled by Swedish Royalty Pro-tection so Erin was absolutely out of the loop and it pained her to have to ask Alexandra.

"I am meeting Nicolas for a walk in the palace grounds shortly, but if you would rather not come, if you aren't feeling well, then it isn't a problem, Nicolas's security will cover me too."

Erin closed her eyes to the pain, recognising that she was being given a way out. But she didn't want to sit for any more hours in her room imagining the worst. Alexandra had said she loved her last night. Said it so many times. Then Alexandra had made love to her. Made her feel like the most special person in the world to her. Yet, this morning she would be spending time with her future husband. Erin felt sick to the stomach.

"I er.... I think I should come along. The fresh air will do me good."

"Okay, well we leave at 12."

"Nicolas," Alexandra beamed a welcome to him. Nicolas smiled and kissed her cheek delicately.

"Princess. You look beautiful this morning."

They walked together across the grounds. Erin sat in a Range Rover at a distance with the Prince's security, sunglasses hid her red eyes while she tried to block out their loud Swedish chatter.

"Do you know the history of our palace, Alexandra? Well, this was where both myself, my father, grandfather and great grandfather were born. I grew up here. I always loved it here. We have very lovely grounds that I used to play in as a boy. I was thinking, today, we could walk the grounds together. I would love to tell you all about the history of the palace. I have had a picnic ordered for us that will be delivered to us in a while, we can sit and enjoy this lovely weather. Afterwards, depending on your feelings, we can venture out of the palace gates and I can contact our media advisor who can ensure we get photographed together in the public park and these photos be distributed to the world's media. Dependent entirely on your wishes. Please, I will not be offended at all if you choose not to or you aren't ready for that level of exposure."

Alexandra knew that this was the next step, she knew that this was what she had to do. She also realised that she liked Nicolas. She liked his quiet respect, his geekiness, she liked to spend time with him.

"Nicolas, I have carefully considered what you have said to me, and I would like to progress with things, ideally moving towards a public announcement of our engagement. So yes, absolutely, please do organise for photos in the public park."

"How wonderful, Alexandra, I am so pleased you have accepted my suggestion. Give me a second." He reached to his pocket for his phone and dialled his advisor. "Please go ahead with the photos planned for the afternoon, please get the necessary journalists in place."

They sat for a picnic in the sunshine, the setting idyllic. At least it would have been if Alexandra couldn't feel Erin's eyes burning through her from a distance. Erin was going to have to get used to this somehow. But, how? Was it fair to ask her to? If she really loved her, was it fair to ask this of her? To drag Erin into her fucked up world and ask her to live as a dirty secret?

Alexandra, who usually planned things so carefully, had not planned on falling in love with her bodyguard.

20

E rin left the Range Rover as the Princess and Prince left the gates of the palace and headed out into the big public city park next to the palace. She would work on foot now, on radio contact with the rest of the security team. Following at a distance. Close enough to move quickly in case of a problem, far enough away to give the couple their privacy.

She watched as journalists showed up, she had been informed of the situation along with the rest of the security team over the radio. She gritted her teeth as she watched Alexandra's perfectly manicured right hand reach for the hand of the Prince. Alexandra in a lovely fitted summery dress in periwinkle blue. The Prince, ever smart, in slacks and an open neck shirt. They walked hand in hand through the park, Erin following at a respectful distance, sick deep in her stomach.

Tears pricked at Erin's eyes. She was ever grateful she had chosen to wear sunglasses. This wasn't how she thought it would be. She thought that she would be ok with seeing Alexandra like this. She had known the situation all along. The truth of who Alexandra was and the way she was forced to live. Erin's dreams late at night were a naive hope that she could run away and live happily ever with the future Queen. What did she want Alexandra to do? Walk away from all her responsibilities?

Erin had been foolish to fall in love with the Princess. Rule number one of her job was to remain professional. Professional was not falling in love or fucking the client. Alexandra had spent last night telling her how much she loved her. But the love of the Princess was the most painful love that there was.

Nicolas and Alexandra sat on a bench in the park and he leaned across and kissed her lovely cheek and the cameras of the world went wild. They barely had had anything on Alexandra's love life in sixteen years since she had turned eighteen. Some public appearances with Lord Hugo that never seemed to go anywhere. Here was this new delicate love they saw in Alexandra with the handsome prince. Alexandra was right, it was everything the public wanted.

How much more would they take from her? How much more was she prepared to give?

THAT EVENING, safely ensconced back in their respective rooms and the staff dismissed, Erin's phone beeped. It was Alexandra.

Come to me.

It never usually pained her, but it pained her now, to be summoned like a dog and to have to go. To want to go and to not want to go all at once, but the Princess was her job and when summoned, she had to go.

She opened the door to Alexandra's rooms and walked in. Alexandra was still in the pretty summer dress, it clung to her full breasts and tiny waist and then flowed out like a ballerina or a fairy. She stood by the window, bathed in golden light from the setting sun.

"Take a seat," she said.

Erin sat on the ornate sofa. It was decorative rather than comfy, but it didn't matter. Nothing really mattered now. She put her head in her hands.

"I don't think I can do this," Erin mumbled into her hands. "I knew the score. Of course I did. But I had no idea it would hurt this much."

"I'm so sorry, Erin." Alexandra remained at a distance. They both knew what would happen if they got too close. "I wish things could be different. There is a way for us to work, you know. If you can find a way to accept the rest of my life. My commitments. The things that I have to do that are so much bigger than myself and my own desires."

Alexandra sighed and looked out of the window. Looking at Erin was perhaps too painful.

"I have been cruel to you. To draw you into my difficult life and hope that you could become a part of it. I realise how much I have asked of you, and for that, I am sorry. I've been selfish in pursuing you and falling in love with you. I am so so very sorry Erin. Please tell me what it is that you need."

I need you. I need you. I need you. I love you.

Erin thoughts were loud in her head. But she swallowed the words.

"I need space. I'll do my job. I want to continue my job. Getting the opportunity to work for you has been the best thing that ever happened to me. But I don't want to see you outside of that." Erin couldn't look at her, so she looked at the floor. "I want us to remain professional, Ma'am."

It hurt Alexandra to hear the use of Ma'am with nobody else around. It hurt Alexandra to realise what was happening here. That the woman she loved was ending things. This wasn't how she saw this going.

"Then, you are dismissed, Sergeant Kennedy," she said into the window, every word an effort. "Thank you for your time."

Erin scuttled out of the room as fast as she could.

Alexandra collapsed to the floor in tears. A distress on a level she had never known. She was suddenly sobbing so hard that she couldn't stop. She felt as though her heart had been ripped out of her body. The pain in her chest overwhelmed her. She lay foetal on the floor hugging her knees to her chest as the tears kept coming. She couldn't breathe. She gasped for breath as the pain racked her body. She coughed. She coughed more and ran to the bath-room as she made herself sick with the coughing.

She crawled back towards the sofa and grabbed the phone in the room.

"Hello," she gasped between sobs. "This

is Princess Alexandra. I think I need a doctor."

"Of course Ma'am." The voice on the other end of the line was immediately concerned. "Right away. Can I send someone for you before the doctor arrives?"

Erin, Erin, she needed Erin.

Her parents? God, no.

"Alicia," she choked. "Alicia." Then she dropped the phone as she hyperventilated.

Alicia's room was close and she let herself in quickly to find Alexandra a mess panicking on the floor.

"I can't breathe," she sobbed.

Alicia had a moment of shock. Never in years of doing the Princess's hair and make up had she seen anything but smiles and professionalism from her. So gathered. So together. So level headed and calm.

"Ma'am. It's okay, I am here. A doctor is coming." Alicia sat immediately on the floor behind, legs wide around her and pulled her into her arms and comforted her like a baby.

Alicia had seen pain and felt heartbreak before. That absolutely had to be what this was. Nothing else hurt like heartbreak. But Nicolas? Surely not. Just this afternoon, the photos in the park, things couldn't have been better between them. Having said that, Alicia hadn't ever thought Alexandra was that into Nicolas. There must be someone else. But, who? Surely Alicia would have noticed if the Princess was seeing someone else.

Alicia rocked her and shushed her and said soothing things but the Princess couldn't stop the sobbing, the choking, the inability to breathe.

"My chest hurts. So much."

"I know, I know Ma'am, it will be ok. The doctor will be here soon."

A firm knock at the door.

"Come in," shouted Alicia.

The doctor was smart in a suit, despite the late hour. He was the Swedish Palace Doctor, but his English was impeccable.

"She's panicking, she can't breathe. She keeps choking." Alicia said.

Alexandra sobbed more.

"Has something serious happened?" asked the doctor. "Has she received bad news."

"I have no idea," said Alicia. "She was like this when I got here."

"Ma'am, I'm Sven Erikson. I am the Doctor. May I touch your wrist to take your pulse?"

Alexandra nodded consent and Erikson held her delicate wrist as he counted the beats.

"Ma'am, there is nothing on your medical history to indicate anything sinister is going on here."

"Did you receive some bad news?"

Alexandra nodded again between gasping.

"Okay, Ma'am, I want you to look at me, focus on me. This is a panic attack you are having in response to trauma. I need you to sit up, try and focus."

Alicia helped her into a sitting position.

"That is good," the doctor said calmly. "Now I need you to focus on me and focus on deep breaths. You need to realise that this is a panic attack and stay calm. Breathe with me. In... 1 second and 2 seconds. Out 1 second and 2 seconds. Good."

Within minutes the doctor helped Alexandra regain control of her breathing, but the tears wouldn't stop rolling from her deep blue eyes.

"My heart, is my heart ok? It hurts so much."

"Ma'am, sometimes we feel mental pain in a physical manner. It is quite common for a panic attack to feel like a heart attack. You've never had panic attacks before?"

She shook her head.

"Something has clearly upset you badly. You will be ok though. Just focus on breathing deeply and calmly if you start to lose control of breathing again."

"Can you stay with her tonight?" he looked to Alicia. "Ma'am, you shouldn't be alone tonight."

"Of course." Alicia nodded. "I'll look after her." Alicia remembered her own broken hearts over the years, and those of her best friends. Sometimes, when it was bad like this, you just needed someone to care for you and help you through it.

The doctor left and Alicia sat up through the night. Alexandra lay across her lap on the sofa and Alicia stroked her hair and reassured her as she sobbed. The tears began to run dry eventually but Alexandra continued to whimper and yelp in pain.

Alexandra had never felt true heartbreak before and had never known pain like it.

Erin, I can't breathe without you.

21

The next morning Alicia helped Alexandra shower and dress ready for the flight back to London.

The official story was that Alexandra had suffered a migraine last night. She didn't want to speak with anyone today and Alicia would protect her from that and sit next to her on the flight. Alexandra was glad of dark glasses that Alicia lent her to cover her red raw eyes and hide further tears. She closed her eyes when she saw Erin in passing and headed straight to the back seat of the Range Rover clinging to Alicia as they both climbed into the back seat.

The flight was similar. Alexandra sat with Alicia and closed her eyes. Back in London, back to the palace, Alexandra was numb and mute and so grateful to Alicia who fended off everyone for her.

She stayed in her room for days and had all her engagements cancelled for her. The British Royal Family doctor was called for her repeatedly and couldn't find anything physically wrong with her and said she just needed time.

Alexandra never took time off and was never sick, so the palace gave her the space she requested.

Erin meanwhile, spent so much time alone in her room. Imagining Alexandra in her own room, no idea what this time off was really about. She had heard about Alexandra's migraine in Sweden, but she had also heard from the British doctor who was visiting her regularly that there was nothing serious wrong with her. Erin was relieved at that, but unsure what to do. She had been given time off, but she had no idea what to do with it. She remained at the palace, just in case Alexandra decided she wanted to go somewhere.

She felt relief at moving their relationship back to purely professional. It was easier for her to detach and just do the job. She didn't know how much it might affect her having to still see the Princess, but she thought she could do it. If Alexandra ever emerged from her rooms, that was.

~

ALEXANDRA HAD SPENT two weeks catatonic in her apartment refusing to see anyone, with Jess and Alicia fussing round her.

She hadn't really spoken a word and Jess and Alicia knew better than to pry.

"I'd like to see Prince Nicolas," she said out of nowhere one morning.

"Sure," responded Jess, ever efficient. "I will make it happen. You want him to come here?"

Alexandra nodded, gazing into the distance.

"Of course." Jess hurried off, eager to make it happen.

~

NICOLAS FLEW in the next day, keen to speak to Alexandra. He hadn't heard from her since her visit to Sweden and he was worried. But he respected her decision to be left alone. He understood she was unwell and perhaps needed some time. He arrived at the palace, curious as everyone else to find out what was happening.

Alexandra waited in her drawing room to receive Nicolas. Alicia had done the best she could and made her up naturally, doing what she could to hide the bags under her eyes and the gaunt look on her face. Alexandra wore a simple green dress, which hung off her slightly now. Heartbreak has always been a fast weight loss solution.

Nicolas arrived and greeted Alexandra warmly. He kissed both her cheeks. Jess scurried around serving them both drinks and sandwiches and then left them alone.

"Nicolas, I want to thank you so much for coming all this way just to see me. I know you have given me every opportunity to speak openly and honestly with you and you have shown me every respect. And yet, I have remained guarded, I haven't shared my secrets and for that I am sorry. I need to be honest with you now."

"Alexandra, you have no need to thank me or apologise. We all have our secrets, it is the nature of being a royal. We choose to share if and when we need to."

"I know. And I need to now. I have realised over the past couple of weeks that I cannot go on feeling like this. I have never told anyone this before, but I trust you implicitly. I welcome your advice."

"Go on," Nicolas was warm and open and respectful and Alexandra was eternally grateful for that.

"I haven't married yet, because I'm not interested in men. It is women that I love and only women. I always have. I am gay."

"Oh Alexandra. I'm so honoured you felt you could share with me. It is your bodyguard isn't it. The one with the dark hair? She is the woman you love?"

"How did you know?" Alexandra raised her head.

"I saw the way you looked at her. I may not say a lot, but I see a lot. This is the cause of your pain isn't it? This forbidden love?"

"I'm so sorry."

"Alexandra, please do not apologise for who you are. Please do not apologise for hurting me. We are friends. I welcome your honesty."

"What do I do now though?" Alexandra looked to him intently, realising that perhaps he was right in that they had become friends over the past few months. She did trust him. She was speaking openly with him as normal people did with their friends.

"Oh, my darling. I see your pain. I will stand by you through this. You have a couple of options as I see it. Firstly, you can carry on with your marriage to me and I will keep your secrets for you. You would be very welcome to have her live with us and I will give you both all the privacy and respect in the world. But honestly, Alexandra, I see the pain in your eyes. I'm not sure you can continue living a double life, it is killing you. It is 2022 Alexandra, you could come out. You are in a position of great power. I know you think your father holds the power and you need to please him, but really he doesn't. You are the future of the monarchy. You are one of the most adored women in the world. You can make this choice to come out. There is gay royalty out there. There will be more in the future. Of that I am sure. Yes, you would, of course be the most high profile Royal to come out. But you would pave the way for the future. You would be an ambassador, a role model. You would be authentic to yourself and that will bring out the real light within you. Think about it, Alexandra. I will meet with your parents and their advisors with you and support you if it is something you want to do. But I see it in you, such a big, bold part of you. You could do so much good here, for yourself and for others. You love this bodyguard don't you?"

"Yes. Very much."

"What is her name?"

"It's Erin Kennedy."

"Does Erin love you too?"

"I think so."

"Don't let Erin go Alexandra. Don't ruin the most precious thing you have, the thing that makes you happier than anything else in the world. Fight for her, for your love. Be braver. Make the difficult choices. Stand up for what I know you believe in. Do you want to live in a world where being gay is a dirty secret? Do you want other women to feel trapped the way you have for years? You can make this difference. You and Erin can be the golden couple. You can change the world for the the better."

Alexandra sat for a minute thinking and then she smiled. For the first time in weeks.

"Thank you, Nicolas." She grasped his hand in gratitude. "Thank you so much. You don't know how much this means to me, I will never forget it."

"JESS," she shouted and Jess bustled in quickly. "Please arrange a meeting with my mother, father and their advisors as soon as possible please. That will be everything."

"Of course," said Jess and she was straight out of the door and on with it.

Nicolas smiled. "You are doing the right thing. I will come with you. It will all be okay."

22

F inally, Erin had a schedule. Alexandra was visiting the country residence. The impressive castle that Erin used to work residential security on. The plan was to stay a couple of days. She still had heard nothing from Alexandra on a personal level, but she hadn't expected to after what she had requested.

Completely professional, Erin waited outside the drawing room ready for 12 o' clock when Alexandra was designated to move.

Alexandra swept out, not looking to her and Erin fell in step behind her. It was a job, just a job, she could do it.

"Kennedy to Asher. Rose is on the move as per schedule. Over." Erin spoke confidently to her radio microphone. She would do her job perfectly.

"Roger that, Kennedy." The response came.

They made it safely into the vehicles, Alexandra on the back seat with sunglasses on, quiet.

The journey passed uneventfully.

What are you thinking Alex?

THEY HAD ARRIVED at the castle early afternoon and Alexandra had no plans, she had gone straight to her room. Erin was lounging in her designated room, reading.

It was early evening when most of the staff had gone home when Erin's phone beeped. Alexandra.

Meet me by the rose garden at 8pm.

Erin looked at her phone, slightly confused. Why would she not just walk out with the Princess if Alexandra wanted to walk? Why meet her there? Ok well, she must have something going on with the other security if she was in the castle grounds already by herself. How was she supposed to do her job properly if Alexandra was going to undermine her like this?

She looked at her watch. 7.45. She replied to the message:

Sure

Erin jumped in the shower. She had been wearing the same clothes all day. A quick wash and dry and she popped her tight black jeans on and a casual t shirt. It was a warm evening and they weren't leaving the grounds. Surely a T shirt would be fine and nothing more formal would be required.

She headed down to the rose garden. It was magnificent. This one was far better than the one at the palace in London. It was much larger, with elaborate archways of beautiful roses and paths honeycombing through it.

She could smell the roses before she got close. Alexandra was there, radiant in a floaty pink summer dress, her ashy blonde hair in loose waves, it had grown just past her shoulders now. Her dress was cerise pink, like some of the roses. It nipped in at the waist and Erin instantly thought she looked even thinner than usual. Her breasts less full, her arms looked skinny. But beautiful. Alexandra was always so so beautiful.

Alexandra met her eyes for the first time since that night. Her blue gaze burning into Erin's very soul.

"Walk with me?" she requested.

Erin fell into step behind her as her training dictated.

"Alongside me." Alexandra clarified.

Erin moved up beside her and walked with her through the roses. There was peace and there was beauty and there were minutes before she spoke.

"I do not have the words to tell you how sorry I am for the pain that I have caused you." Alexandra began as they continued to walk. "I have a lot to tell you and I don't really know where to start."

Erin looked to her, curious.

Alexandra took Erin's hand, turned to her and took her other hand. She looked deep into Erin's dark eyes and saw the toll the past couple of weeks had taken on her too.

"I love you, Erin. Completely and absolutely." Erin looked shocked. "I cannot be without you. I cannot breathe without you. I want you back. Officially though. I am going to come out."

Erin stood absolutely stunned and speechless, her T shirt tight around her biceps.

"Also, you look totally hot in this T shirt. Please wear it more often." Alexandra laughed and wormed her small hands into the waistband of Erin's jeans. As her fingers touched the skin on Erin's hips she felt alive again.

"I love you, Erin. I adore you. We are going to be together. I have come out to my family and I want to come out publicly. My father has given us this castle as our home. If you like it? If you want it? It is ours. We can have all the horses here. We can get a dog. We can live a beautiful life. If you want to? If you can forgive me. You have lit a fire in me that will never die. You have shown me what real love is. Let me love you back. Properly. Say something, please."

"What about Nicolas?" Erin asked.

"It is over. I cannot marry someone I am not in love with as it turns out. I want you Erin. I want it all with you."

"Your parents?"

"I think they understand. Finally. Nicolas helped me make them understand. It isn't perhaps the route they would have chosen for me, but they've taken it surprisingly well. You've been checked out, of course. By Henry. Even deeper checks than were first done when you started working for me have been done over the past couple of days. Your family, your friends, your whole life has been analysed, I'm afraid. But the good news is that you passed their tests. There's nothing scandalous that would be damaging to me. And your family are way more middle class than you made out." She laughed.

Erin felt suddenly weak at the knees and sat on a nearby bench.

"I can't believe this. Seriously, I cant. I

mean, this is more than I ever hoped for. I feel like I am in a dream."

"It is no dream." Alexandra sat astride Erin on the bench, held her face and kissed her deeply.

Erin felt her body responding, felt the pain of the past weeks fading. Alexandra was hers, only hers. She was going to come out. They were going to be together properly. Alexandra's tongue met her own.

She reached instinctively between Alexandra's legs, the floaty dress providing ease of access and was met by silk panties. Very wet silk panties. She brushed underneath them feeling Alexandra's heat before Alexandra pulled her hand away.

"Later," she whispered in Erin's ear. "Later I will give you all of me and take all of you. We have all the time in the world. But first, there's something else." She smiled like a naughty teenager.

Erin gripped her wrists tightly and looked into the loveliness of her face.

"I love you, Alex. More than I ever thought was possible. You are incredible, intelligent and beautiful, and every day I want you more. You are my sunshine. Yes.

Yes to everything you are asking. A million yeses. I want to spend the rest of my life loving you."

Erin kissed her like it was the first time again and as they both came out of the kiss, Alexandra jumped up and took her hand leading her through another tunnel of roses.

They came out to a table and chairs and a waitress in the clearing of the garden.

"Ma'am," the waitress curtsied her respect.

She pulled Alexandra's chair out to seat her and then the same for Erin.

She lifted the lids on plate after plate of beautiful food.

She served them both with a cold, fruity Sangria that tasted incredible.

Alexandra smiled across the table at her.

"This is our second date, my love. Soho was the first, although I think I forgot to mention that it was a date at the time." She winked. "Try not to hit anyone on this date."

"I was just wondering if Princess's put out on second dates?" Erin smirked.

"Oh this one will. All night long."

They both laughed and held hands across the table.

"I'm so in love with you Erin. I'm not sure how easy coming out will be, but it will be a whole lot easier with you by my side and your strong arms to always come home to. I can only thank you for setting me free from the cage I had put myself in."

"You are doing the right thing Alex. Coming out might be hard, but you will never look back. I've got you, through it all, I promise."

And Alexandra knew that she did. She knew that Erin would be her rock throughout this and her future challenges.

"The only thing is, if you are officially my girlfriend, I'm going to need a new bodyguard!" she laughed.

Erin laughed with her. She was ready to follow Alexandra in her new capacity as girlfriend. Ready to love her through it all.

EPILOGUE

Princess Alexandra stood in front of a packed outdoor press conference in the sun in the gardens of the castle and spoke to the press and to the world. Her coming out played live on television throughout the world. Every news station in the world wanted a piece of her.

"People of the United Kingdom, Commonwealth Realms and the world. I know you have all eagerly awaited news of my engagement and that this might come as a shock to a lot of you. I have chosen to speak today myself. The royal advisors wanted our press secretary to speak for me, but the least I can give you is my honesty in person."

Her eyes were intent as they looked into the cameras, her face serious and her hair lifted slightly in the breeze. The rich blue dress they had put her in was the colour she always suited best, befitting of Alexandra the Princess and Alexandra the person.

"I want you to see me today, not just as your Princess and future Queen, but as Alexandra. Alexandra the person. Behind everything I do to serve, there is a person and her name is Alexandra. For so long, I felt such a weight of expectation to marry and bear children, not out of love, but out of duty, and late at night, I used to cry alone in my bed.

I have hidden a huge part of myself and that is not the way I choose to live. That has gone against everything I believe in and everything that I am.

I need you all to know that, whilst I respect him greatly and have become great friends with him, I will NOT be announcing my engagement to Prince Nicolas. I will not now, or ever be announcing my engagement to any man. I love women, and only women, I always have."

There were gasps through the crowd of journalists. It clearly wasn't what they were expecting, but they gave her the respect and remained transfixed on her as she continued.

"I wish that I lived in a world where I hadn't carried this burden of my sexuality in secrecy and silence for thirty five years. I wish I had been braver, years ago, braver and more honest with myself and with the world. But, I cannot change the past. I want to change things for the better. I want this to be the start of a brighter future. I want no young girl or boy to feel trapped like I did, for so long. I want to change things in countries where it is illegal to be gay and campaign for a better world for all of us."

Alexandra fixed her ocean eyes into the cameras.

"Mostly, I want to continue to do good. To help people. To serve. If my coming out helps one person who is struggling with their sexuality, then it was worth it."

She took a deep breath.

"I was born into this role, and it is a role

I have taken and will continue to take very seriously. I want to thank you all for your continued support of myself and the Royal family throughout my life. I want to thank my parents for their support in this decision I have made to come out. I know it has been difficult for them to amend the expectations they had for their only daughter, and indeed the expectations that for centuries have been put upon royalty. I will continue to support all the causes and charities that believe in so greatly. I will continue to fight for a better world for all of us. I will continue to do good."

There was a moment of silence while everyone took in her words before she spoke again.

"I will take a couple of questions now, if you have any."

The journalists went immediately mad, shouting, waving their hands.

"Princess!"

"Ma'am!"

"Alexandra!"

Alexandra pointed confidently at a young woman who introduced herself.

"Ruby Costello, BBC. Ma'am, can you

tell us if you still plan to have children and if so, how?"

"Thank you Ruby, yes, all being well, I do still plan to have children. I haven't made any definitive decisions yet on how, but I'm sure you know as well as I do that there are many options out there these days."

Alexandra pointed to another journalist with his hand up.

"Peter Johnson, The Daily Mail."

Alexandra sighed inwardly knowing his question could be anything. The newspaper he wrote for was full of unsubstantiated gossip.

"Go ahead, Peter."

"Ma'am can you confirm the rumours that you have been sleeping with your bodyguard?"

Alexandra smiled wryly, wondering how it had got out, but she had discussed the potential of this question at length with her advisors and with Erin herself. Once Erin's name got out there, her privacy and that of her family would be a thing of the past.

The journalists all turned their heads in

surprise at the question. None of them expected any answer other than denial.

"I can confirm that my girlfriend is my ex bodyguard Sergeant Erin Kennedy and I love her very much. For obvious reasons, she is no longer working as part of my protection team. We will be appearing together at some point, very soon, to enable you all to get some photographs, but meanwhile if you could give our home, the castle, some privacy, I would very much appreciate it. Erin has given me so much that I will be eternally grateful for. Mostly she has given me the ability to be authentically myself, Alexandra. In encouraging me to come out, she has given me a freedom that I never thought I could have."

The journalists gasped and lapped it up.

ERIN SMILED, watching her girlfriend on television, addressing the world about their relationship. Alex was confident and eloquent. Erin saw the burden fall, piece by piece, from her shoulders with every word that she said. Alex was incredible and the way the light lit up her lovely face filled Erin with warmth. She sat happily in their amazing home in the castle with their tired Great Dane puppy, Audrey, lying across her lap.

Alex, I love you too.
THE END

HER ROYAL BODYGUARD
BOOK 2

The sequel to Her Royal Bodyguard following Erin and Princess Alexandra further is available to order now. Click the following link or type the following into your web browser to order your copy now.

getbook.at/HRB2

~

THANK YOU!

Hey everyone, I just want to thank you so much for reading my book. I would love for you to pop on Amazon and review it if you enjoyed it. As an indie author, reviews really do make a difference and get my books noticed and would be hugely appreciated.

I wrote Her Royal Bodyguard following my own experience as a bodyguard (Close Protection Operative) to a member of a Royal Family. (It wasn't the British Royal Family.) Being a Bodyguard isn't as glamorous as you

might think. It is a lonely, isolating profession. You give up your own life to live in the client's world as their shadow. Working so closely for someone over time, with their safety your absolute priority, you develop a certain intimacy with them. Although I didn't have an affair with my Princess (Sorry to disappoint!), I can see how easily it could happen.

～

Mailing List

You can join my mailing list by going to my website and filling in your email address. Keep up to date with new releases and special offers and free books :)
www.lovefrommargaux.com

～

Go give me a follow on Social Media and don't be afraid to give me any feedback on anything you particularly enjoyed or didn't enjoy about the book.

www.facebook.com/lovefrommargaux

www.instagram.com/lovefrommargaux

www.twitter.com/lovefrommargaux

Or contact me on email:
lovefrommargaux@hotmail.com

Please also check out my other books. All my books are available to read for free on Kindle Unlimited.

ALSO BY MARGAUX FOX

FREE BOOK:

Get this FREE second chance romance when you sign up to my mailing list at the following link. Can Shay get a second chance with the woman who was cruelly torn away from her?

https://BookHip.com/NGSVJP

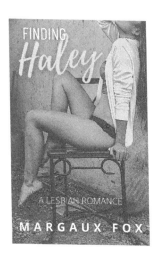

Following the breakdown of her marriage,
Haley runs away to a sunny beach paradise to
find herself. Will she find herself in the arms of
a seductive older woman?

getbook.at/Haley

Can you find love with someone from a different world?

getbook.at/Lilysworld

Will Diana be able to resist the charms of her seductive young intern?

getbook.at/HLI

Jen is blown away by attention from the
enigmatic stranger, Lyra. What does Lyra want
with someone ordinary like her?

getbook.at/FFH

Jo and Carole were each other's first love as teenagers. Can they recapture the magic they once had after 25 years of pain and loss?

getbook.at/HCC

Printed in Great Britain
by Amazon

59239424R00142